John Hawkesworth

Almoran and Hamet

An Oriental tale: Volume 2

John Hawkesworth

Almoran and Hamet
An Oriental tale: Volume 2

ISBN/EAN: 9783337335380

Printed in Europe, USA, Canada, Australia, Japan

Cover: Foto ©Andreas Hilbeck / pixelio.de

More available books at **www.hansebooks.com**

ALMORAN

AND

HAMET:

AN

ORIENTAL TALE.

In TWO VOLUMES.

VOLUME SECOND.

LONDON:

Printed for H. Payne, and W. Cropley,
at Dryden's Head in Pater-noster Row.
MDCCLXI.

ALMORAN

AND

HAMET.

✿✿✿✿✿✿✿✿✿✿✿✿✿✿✿✿✿✿✿✿✿✿✿✿✿

CHAP. XI.

ALMORAN had now reached the gallery; and when the multitude faw him, they fhouted as in triumph, and demanded that he fhould furrender. HAMET, who alfo perceived him at a diftance, and was unwilling that any violence fhould be offered to

his

his perfon, preffed forward, and when he was come near, commanded filence. At this moment ALMORAN, with a loud voice, reproached them with impiety and folly; and appealing to the power, whom in his perfon they had offended, the air fuddenly grew dark, a flood of lightning defcended from the fky, and a peal of thunder was articulated into thefe words:

Divided fway, the God who reigns alone
Abhors; and gives to ALMORAN the throne.

The multitude ftood aghaft at the prodigy; and hiding their faces with their hands, every one departed in filence and confufion, and HAMET and OMAR were left alone. OMAR was taken by fome of the foldiers who had

adhered

adhered to ALMORAN, but HAMET made his efcape.

ALMORAN, whofe wifhes were thus far accomplifhed by the intervention of a power fuperior to his own, exulted in the anticipation of that happinefs which he now fuppofed to be fecured; and was fortified in his opinion, that he had been wretched only becaufe he had been weak, and that to multiply and not to fupprefs his wifhes was the way to acquire felicity.

As he was returning from the gallery, he was met by Ofmyn and Caled, who had heard the fupernatural declaration in his behalf, and learned its effects. ALMORAN, in that hafty flow of un-bounded but capricious favour, which,

in

in contracted minds, is the effect only
of unexpected good fortune, raised
Ofmyn from his feet to his bofom:
' As in the trial,' faid he, ' thou haft
' been faithful, I now inveft thee with
' a fuperior truft. The toils of ftate
' fhall from this moment devolve
' upon thee; and from this moment,
' the delights of empire unallayed fhall
' be mine: I will recline at eafe, re-
' mote from every eye but thofe that
' reflect my own felicity; the felicity
' that I fhall tafte in fecret, furround-
' ed by the fmiles of beauty, and the
' gaities of youth. Like heaven, I
' will reign unfeen; and like heaven,
' though unfeen, I will be adored.'
Ofmyn received this delegation of
power with a tumultuous pleafure, that
was expreffed only by filence and confufion.

fufion. ALMORAN remarked it; and exulting in the pride of power, he fuddenly changed his afpect, and regarding Ofmyn, who was yet blufhing, and whofe eyes were fwimming in tears of gratitude, with a ftern and ardent countenance; ' Let me, however,' faid he, ' warn thee to be watchful in thy truft: ' beware, that no rude commotion, violate my peace by thy fault; left my ' anger fweep thee in a moment to de-' ftruction.' He then directed his eye to Caled: ' And thou too,' faid he, ' haft been faithful; be thou next in ' honour and in power to Ofmyn. ' Guard both of you my paradife from ' dread and care; fulfill the duty that ' I have affigned you, and live.'

He

He was then informed by a meſſenger, that HAMET had eſcaped, and that OMAR was taken. As he now deſpiſed the power both of HAMET and OMAR, he expreſſed neither concern nor anger that HAMET had fled; but he ordered OMAR to be brought before him.

When OMAR appeared bound and diſarmed, he regarded him with a ſmile of inſult and deriſion; and aſked him, what he had now to hope. ‘ I have, ‘ indeed,’ ſaid OMAR, ‘ much leſs to ‘ hope, than thou haſt to fear.’ ‘ Thy ‘ inſolence,’ ſaid ALMORAN, ‘ is equal ‘ to thy folly: what power on earth is ‘ there, that I ſhould fear?’ ‘ Thy ‘ own,’ ſaid OMAR. ‘ I have not lei- ‘ ſure now,’ replied ALMORAN, ‘ to
‘ hear

' hear the paradoxes of thy philpfophy
' explained : but to fhew thee, that I
' fear not thy power, thou fhalt live.
' I will leave thee to hopelefs regret;
' to wiles that have been fcorned
' and defeated; to the unheeded pe-
' tulance of dotage; to the fondnefs
' that is repayed with neglect; to reft-
' lefs wifhes, to credulous hopes, and
' to derided command : to the flow and
' complicated torture of defpifed old
' age; and that, when thou fhalt long
' have abhorred thy being, fhall deftroy
' it.' ' The mifery,' faid OMAR, ' which
' thou haft menaced, it is not in thy
' power to inflict. As thou haft taken
' from me all that I poffeffed by the
' bounty of thy father, it is true
' that I am poor; it is true alfo, that
' my knees are now feeble, and

B 4   ' bend

' bend with the weight of years that is
' upon me. I am, as thou art, a man;
' and therefore I have erred : but I
' have ftill kept the narrow path in
' view with a faithful vigilance, and to
' that I have foon returned : the paft,
' therefore, I do not regret; 'and the fu-
' ture I have no caufe to fear. 'In Him
' who is moft merciful, I have hope;
' and in that hope even now I rejoice
' before thee. My portion in the pre-
' fent hour, is adverfity : but I receive
' it, not only with humility, but thank-
' fulnefs; for I know, that whatever
' is ordained is beft.'

ALMORAN, in whofe heart there
were no traces of OMAR's virtue, and
therefore no foundation for his confidence; fuftained himfelf againft their
force,

force, by treating them as hypocrify
and affectation : ' I know,' fays he,
' that thou haft long learned to eccho
' the fpecious and pompous founds, by
' which hypocrites conceal their wretch-
' ednefs, and excite the admiration of
' folly and the contempt of wifdom :
' yet thy walk in this place, fhall be
' ftill unreftrained. Here the fplendor of
' my felicity fhall fill thy heart with
' envy, and cover thy face with con-
' fufion; and from thee fhall the world
' be inftructed, that the enemies of
' ALMORAN can move no paffion in his
' breaft but contempt, and that moft
' to punifh them is to permit them to
' live.'

OMAR, whofe eye had till now been
fixed upon the ground, regarded AL-

MORAN

MORAN with a calm but steady countenance: 'Here then,' said he, 'will I 'follow thee, constant as thy shadow; 'tho', as thy shadow, unnoticed or ne- 'glected: here shall mine eye watch 'those evils, that were appointed from 'everlasting to attend upon guilt: and. 'here shall my voice warn thee of 'their approach. From thy breast may 'they be averted by righteousness! for 'without this, though all the worlds 'that roll above thee should, to aid 'thee, unite all their power, that 'power can aid thee only to be 'wretched.'

ALMORAN, in all the pride of gratified ambition, invested with dominion that had no limits, and allied with powers that were more than mortal; was overawed by this addrefs, and his countenance grew pale. But the next moment, difdaining to be thus controuled by the voice of a flave, his cheeks were fuffufed with the blufhes of indignation : he turned from OMAR, in fcorn, anger, and confufion, without reply; and OMAR departed with the calm dignity of a benevolent and fupe-rior being, to whom the fmiles and frowns of terreftrial tyranny were alike indifferent, and in whom abhorrence of the turpitude of vice was mingled with compaffion for its folly.

C H A P.

CHAP. XII.

IN the mean time, ALMEIDA, who had been conveyed to an apartment in ALMORAN's feraglio, and delivered to the care of thofe who attended upon his women, fuffered all that grief and terror could inflict upon a generous, a tender, and a delicate mind; yet in this complicated diftrefs, her attention was principally fixed upon HAMET. The difappointment of his hope, and the violation of his right, were the chief objects of her regret and her fears, in all that had already happened, and in all that was ftill to come; every infult that might be of-

fered

4

fered to herfelf, fhe confidered as an injury to him. Yet the thoughts of all that he might fuffer in her perfon, gave way to her apprehenfions of what might befall him in his own : in his fituation, every calamity that her imagination could conceive, was poffible ; her thoughts were, therefore, bewildered amidft an endlefs variety of dreadful images, which ftarted up before them which way foever they were turned ; and it was impoffible that fhe could gain any certain intelligence of his fate, as the fplendid prifon in which fhe was now confined, was furrounded by mutes and eunuchs, of whom nothing could be learned, or in whofe report no confidence could be placed.

While

While her mind was in this ftate of agitation and diftrefs, fhe perceived the door open, and the next moment ALMORAN entered the apartment. When fhe faw him, fhe turned from him with a look of unutterable anguifh ; and hiding her face in her veil, fhe burft into tears. The tyrant was moved with her diftrefs ; for unfeeling obduracy is the vice only of the old, whofe fenfibility has been worn away by the habitual perpetration of reiterated wrongs.

He approached her with looks of kindnefs, and his voice was involuntarily modulated to pity ; fhe was, however, too much abforbed in her own forrows, to reply. He gazed upon her with tendernefs and admiration ;

tion; and taking her hand into his own, he preffed it ardently to his bofom : his compaffion foon kindled into defire, and from foothing her diltrefs, he began to folicit her love. This inftantly roufed her attention, and refentment now fufpended her grief: fhe turned from him with a firm and haughty ftep, and inftead of anfwering his profeffions, reproached him with her wrongs. ALMORAN, that he might at once addrefs her virtue and her paffions, obferved, that though he had loved her from the firft moment he had feen her, yet he had concealed his paffion even from her, till it had received the fanction of an invifible and fuperior power; that he came, therefore, the meffenger of heaven; and that he offered her unrivalled empire and everlafting love.

love. To this she answered only by an impatient and fond enquiry after HAMET. ' Think not of HAMET,' said ALMORAN; ' for why should he who ' is rejected of Heaven, be still the fa- ' vourite of ALMEIDA?' ' If thy hand,' said ALMEIDA, ' could quench in ' everlasting darkness, that vital spark ' of intellectual fire, which the word ' of the Almighty has kindled in my ' breast to burn for ever, then might ' ALMEIDA cease to think of HAMET; ' but while that shall live, whatever ' form it shall inhabit, or in whatever ' world it shall reside, his image shall ' be for ever present, and to him shall ' my love be for ever true.' This glowing declaration of her love for HA- MET, was immediately succeeded by a tender anxiety for his safety; and a sud-
den

'den reflection upon the probability of his death, and the danger of his situation if alive, threw her again into tears.

ALMORAN, whom the ardour and impetuosity of her passions kept sometimes silent, and sometimes threw into confusion, again attempted to sooth and comfort her : she often urged him to tell her what was become of his brother, and he as often evaded the question. As she was about to renew her enquiry, and reflected that it had already been often made, and had not yet been answered, she thought that AL-MORAN had already put him to death : this threw her into a new agony, of which he did not immediately discover the cause; but as he soon learned it from

her

her reproaches and exclamations, he
perceived that he could not hope to
be heard, while she was in doubt about
the safety of HAMET. In order, therefore, to sooth her mind, and prevent its being longer possessed with an
image that excluded every other; he
assumed a look of concern and astonish-
ment at the imputation of a crime,
which was at once so horrid and so un-
necessary. After a solemn deprecation
of such enormous guilt, he observed,
that as it was now impossible for HA-
MET to succeed as his rival, either in
empire or in love, without the breach
of a command, which he knew his virtue would implicitly obey; he had no
motive either to desire his death, or
to restrain his liberty: ‘ His walk,’
says he, ‘ is still uncircumscribed in
‘ Persia;

' Perfia; and except this chamber,
' there is no part of the palace to
' which he is not admitted.'

To this declaration ALMEIDA liftened, as to the mufic of paradife; and
it fufpended for a-while every paffion,
but her love: the fudden eafe of her
mind made her regardlefs of all about
her, and fhe had in this interval fuffered
ALMORAN to remove her veil, without
reflecting upon what he was doing.
The moment fhe recollected herfelf,
fhe made a gentle effort to recover it,
with fome confufion, but without anger. The pleafure that was expreffed
in her eyes, the blufh that glowed upon her cheek, and the conteft about
the veil, which to an amorous imagination had an air of dalliance, concurred

C 2   to

to heighten the paſſion of ALMORAN almoſt to phrenſy : ſhe perceived her danger in his looks, and her ſpirits inſtantly took the alarm. He ſeized her hand, and gazing ardently upon her, he conjured her, with a tone and emphaſis that ſtrongly expreſſed the tumultuous vehemence of his wiſhes, that ſhe would renounce the rites which had been forbidden above, and that ſhe would receive him to whom by miracle ſhe had been alloted.

ALMEIDA, whom the manner and voice of ALMORAN had terrified into ſilence, anſwered him at firſt only with a look that expreſſed averſion and diſdain, over-awed by fear. ' Wilt thou ' not,' ſaid ALMORAN, ' fulfill the ' decrees of Heaven ? I conjure thee,

' by

' by Heaven, to anfwer.' From this folemn reference to Heaven, ALMEIDA derived new fortitude: fhe inftantly recollefted, that fhe ftood in the prefence of Him, by whofe permiffion only every other power, whether vifible or invifible, can difpenfe evil or good : ' Urge no more,' faid fhe, ' as the decree of Heaven, that ' which is inconfiftent with Divine per-' fection. Can He, in whofe hand ' my heart is, command me to wed ' the man whom he has not enabled me ' to love ? Can the Pure, the Juft, the ' Merciful, have ordained that I fhould ' fuffer embraces which I loath, and ' violate vows which His laws per-' mitted me to make ? Can He ' have ordained a perfidious, a love-' lefs, and a joylefs proftitution ? What

C 3 ' if

' if a thoufand prodigies fhould con-
' cur to enforce it a thoufand times,
' the deed itfelf would be a ftronger
' proof that thofe prodigies were the
' works of darknefs, than thofe prodi-
' gies that the deed was commanded
' by the Father of light.'

ALMORAN, whofe hopes were now
blafted to the root, who perceived that
the virtue of ALMEIDA could neither
be deceived nor overborne; that fhe
at once contemned his power, and abhorred his love; gave way to all the
furies of his mind, which now flum-
bered no more: his countenance expreffed at once anger, indignation, and
defpair; his gefture became furious,
and his voice was loft in menaces and
execrations. ALMEIDA beheld him
with

with an earneſt yet ſteady countenance,
till he vowed to revenge the indignity
he had ſuffered, upon HAMET. At
the name of HAMET, her fortitude for-
ſook her; the pride of virtue gave way
to the ſoftneſs of love; her cheeks became pale, her lips trembled, and taking hold of the robe of ALMORAN,
ſhe threw herſelf at his feet. His fury
was at firſt ſuſpended by hope and expectation; but when from her words,
which grief and terror had rendered
ſcarce articulate, he could learn only
that ſhe was pleading for HAMET, he
burſt from her in an extaſy of rage;
and forcing his robe from her hand,
with a violence that dragged her after
it, he ruſhed out of the chamber, and
left her proſtrate upon the ground.

C 4   As

As he paſſed through the gallery with a haſty and diſordered pace, he was ſeen by OMAR; who knowing that he was returned from an interview with ALMEIDA, and conjecturing from his appearance what had happened, judged that he ought not to neglect this opportunity to warn him once more of the deluſive phantoms, which, under the appearance of pleaſure, were leading him to deſtruction: he, therefore, followed him unperceived, till he had reached the apartment in which he had been uſed to retire alone, and heard again the loud and tumultuous exclamations, which were wrung from his heart by the anguiſh of diſappointment: ' What have I gained,' ſaid he, ' by abſolute dominion! The ſlave ' who, ſecluded from the gales of life

' and

' and from the light of heaven, toils
' without hope in the darknefs of the
' mine, riots in the delights of para-
' dife compared with me. By the ca-
' price of one woman, I am robbed
' not only of enjoyment but of peace,
' and condemned for ever to the tor-
' ment of unfatisfied defire.'

OMAR, who was impatient to apprize him that he was not alone, and
to prevent his difclofing fentiments
which he wifhed to conceal, now threw
himfelf upon the ground at his feet.
' Prefumptuous flave!' faid ALMO-
RAN, ' from whence, and wherefore
' art thou come?' ' I am come,' faid
OMAR, ' to tell thee that not the ca-
' price of a woman, but the wifhes of
' ALMORAN, have made ALMORAN
' wretched.'

'wretched.' The king, ftung with the reproach, drew back, and with a furious look laid his hand upon his poignard; but was immediately reftrained from drawing it, by his pride. 'I am 'come,' faid OMAR, 'to repeat that 'truth, upon which, great as thou art, 'thy fate is fufpended. Thy power 'extends not to the mind of another; 'exert it, therefore, upon thy own: 'fupprefs the wifhes, which thou canft 'not fulfill; and fecure the happinefs 'that is within thy reach.'

ALMORAN, who could bear no longer to hear the precepts which he difdained to practife, fternly commanded OMAR to depart: 'Be gone,' faid he, 'left I crufh thee like a noifome rep- 'tile, which men cannot but abhor,

'though

' though it is too contemptible to be
' feared.'   ' I go,' faid OMAR, ' that
' my warning voice may yet again re-
' call thee to the path of wifdom and
' of peace, if yet again I fhall behold
' thee while it is to be found.'

C H A P.

C H A P. XIII.

ALMORAN was now left alone; and throwing himſelf upon a ſofa, he ſat ſome time motionleſs and ſilent, as if all his faculties had been ſuſpended in the ſtupefaction of deſpair. He revolved in his mind the wiſhes that had been gratified, and the happineſs of which he had been diſappointed: ' I deſired,' ſaid he, ' the pomp ' and power of undivided dominion ; ' and HAMET was driven from the ' throne which he ſhared with me, by ' a voice from heaven : I deſired to ' break off his marriage with ALMEI- ' DA; and it was broken off by a pro- ' digy,

' digy, when no human power could
' have accomplifhed my defire. It was
' my wifh alfo to have the perfon of
' Almeida in my power, and this wifh
' alfo has been gratified; yet I am ftill
' wretched. But I am wretched, only
' becaufe the means have not been ade-
' quate to the end: what I have hi-
' therto obtained, I have not defired
' for itfelf; and of that, for which I
' defired it, I am not poffeffed: I am,
' therefore, ftill wretched, becaufe I
' am weak. With the foul of Almo-
' ran, I fhould have the form of Ha-
' met: then my wifhes would indeed
' be filled; then would Almeida blefs
' me with confenting beauty, and the
' fplendor of my power fhould diftin-
' guifh only the intervals of my love;
' my enjoyments would then be certain

and

' and permanent, neither blasted by
' disappointment, nor withered by sa-
' tiety.' When he had uttered these
reflections with the utmost vehemence
and agitation, his face was again ob-
scured by gloom and despair; his posture was again fixed; and he was fall-
ing back into his former state of silent
abstraction, when he was suddenly
roused by the appearance of the Genius, the sincerity of whose friendship he began to distrust.

' ALMORAN,' said the Genius, ' if
' thou art not yet happy, know that
' my powers are not yet exhausted:
' fear me not, but let thine ear be at-
' tentive to my voice.' The Genius
then stretched out his hand towards
him, in which there was an emerald of
great

great luftre, cut into a figure that had four and twenty fides, on each of which was engraven a different letter. ' Thou ' feeft,' faid he, ' this talifman : on ' each fide of it is engraven one of ' thofe myfterious characters, of which ' are formed all the words of all the ' languages that are fpoken by angels, ' genii, and men. This fhall enable ' thee to change thy figure : and what, ' under the form of ALMORAN, thou ' canft not accomplifh; thou fhalt ftill ' be able to effect, if it can be effected ' by thee, in the form of any other. ' Point only to the letters that com- ' pofe the name of him whofe appear- ' ance thou wouldft affume, and it is ' done. Remember only, that upon ' him, whofe appearance thou fhall af- ' fume, thine fhall be impreft, till thou

' reftoreft

' reftoreft his own. Hide the charm in
' thy bofom, and avail thyfelf of its ˜
' power.' ALMORAN received the talifman in a tranfport of gratitude and
joy, and the Genius immediately difappeared.

The ufe of this talifman was fo obvious, that it was impoffible to overlook
it. ALMORAN inftantly conceived the
defign with which it was given, and
determined inftantly to put it in execution : ' I will now,' faid he, ' af-
' fume the figure of HAMET ; and my
' love, in all its ardour, fhall be return-
' ed by ALMEIDA.' As his fancy kindled at the anticipation of his happinefs,
he ftood mufing in a pleafing fufpenfe,
and indulged himfelf in the contemplation of the feveral gradations, by
which

which he should ascend to the summit of his wishes.

Just at this moment, Ofmyn, whom he had commanded to attend him at this hour, approached his apartment: AL-MORAN was roused by the sound of his foot, and supposed it to be OMAR, who had again intruded upon his privacy; he was enraged at the interruption which had broken a series of imaginations so flattering and luxurious; he snatched out his poignard, and lifting up his arm for the stroke, hastily turned round to have stabbed him; but seeing Ofmyn, he discovered his mistake just in time to prevent the blow.

Ofmyn, who was not conscious of any crime, nor indeed of any act that

D could

could have given occasion of offence; started back terrified and amazed, and stood trembling in suspense whether to remain or to withdraw. ALMORAN, in the mean time, sheathed the instrument of death, and bid him fear nothing, for he should not be hurt. He then turned about; and putting his hand to his forehead, stood again silent in a musing posture: he recollected, that if he assumed the figure of HAMET, it was necessary he should give orders for HAMET to be admitted to ALMEIDA, as he would otherwise be excluded by the delegates of his own authority; turning, therefore, to Ofmyn, ' Remember,' said he, ' that ' whenever HAMET shall return, it is ' my command, that he be admitted to ' ALMEIDA.'

Ofmyn,

Ofmyn, who was pleafed with an opportunity of recommending himfelf to ALMORAN, by praifing an act of ge-nerous virtue which he fuppofed him now to exert in favour of his brother, received the command with a look, that expreffed not only approbation but joy: ' Let the fword of deftruction,' faid he, ' be the guard of the tyrant; ' the ftrength of my lord fhall be the ' bonds of love: thofe, who honour ' thee as ALMORAN, fhall rejoice in ' thee as the friend of HAMET.' To ALMORAN, who was confcious to no kindnefs for his brother, the praife of Ofmyn was a reproach: he was offend-ed at the joy which he faw kindled in his countenance, by a command to fhew favour to HAMET; and was fired

with

with fudden rage at that condemnation
of his real conduct, which was implied
by an encomium on the generofity of
which he affumed the appearance for a
malevolent and perfidious purpofe: his
brow was contracted, his lip quivered,
and the hilt of his dagger was again
grafped in his hand. Ofmyn was again
overwhelmed with terror and confufion;
he had again offended, but knew not his
offence. In the mean time, ALMORAN
recollecting that to exprefs difpleafure
againft Ofmyn was to betray his own
fecret, endeavoured to fupprefs his anger; but his anger was fucceeded by
remorfe, regret, and difappointment.
The anguifh of his mind broke out in
imperfect murmurs: ' What I am,
faid he, ' is, to this wretch, the object
' not only of hatred but of fcorn; and
' he

' he commends only what I am not,
' in what to him I would feem to be.'

Thefe founds, which, tho' not articulate, were yet uttered with great emotion, were ftill miftaken by Ofmyn for the overflowings of capricious and caufelefs anger: ' My life,' fays he to himfelf, ' is even now fufpend-
' ed in a doubtful balance. When-
' ever I approach this tyrant, I tread
' the borders of deftruction : like a
' hood-winked wretch, who is left to
' wander near the brink of a precipice,
' I know my danger; but which way
' foever I turn, I know not whether I
' fhall incur or avoid it.'

In thefe reflections, did the fovereign and the flave pafs thofe moments,

in

in which the fovereign intended to render the flave fubfervient to his pleafure or his fecurity, and the flave intended to exprefs a zeal which he really felt, and a homage which his heart had already paid. Ofmyn was at length, however, difmiffed with an affurance, that all was well; and ALMORAN was again left to reflect with anguifh upon the paft, to regret the prefent, and to anticipate the future with folicitude, anxiety, and perturbation.

He was, however, determined to affume the figure of his brother, by the talifman which had been put into his power by the Genius: but juft as he was about to form the fpell, he recollected, that by the fame act he would imprefs his own likenefs upon HAMET, who

who would confequently be invefted
with his power, and might ufe it to his
deftruction. This held him fome time
in fufpenfe: but reflecting that HA-
MET might not, perhaps, be apprized
of his advantage, till it was too late to
improve it; that he was now a fugitive, and probably alone, leaving Perfia behind him with all the fpeed he
could make; and that, at the worft,
if he fhould be ftill near, if he fhould
know the transformation as foon as it
fhould be made, and fhould inftantly
take the moft effectual meafures to improve it; yet as he could diffolve the
charm in a moment, whenever it fhould
be neceffary for his fafety, no formi-
dable danger could be incurred by the
experiment, to which he, therefore,
proceeded without delay.

D 4   C H A P.

C H A P. XIV.

IN the mean time, HAMET, to whom his own safety was of no importance but for the fake of ALMEIDA, refolved, if poffible, to conceal himfelf near the city. Having, therefore, reached the confines of the defert, by which it was bounded on the eaft, he quitted his horfe, and determined to remain there till the multitude was difperfed, and the darknefs of the evening might conceal his return, when in lefs than an hour he could reach the palace.

He fat down at the foot of the mountain Kabeffed, without confider-
ing,

ing, that in this place he was moſt like-
ly to be found, as thoſe who travel the
deſert ſeldom fail to enter the cave that
winds its way under the mountain, to
drink of the water that iſſues there
from a clear and copious ſpring.

He reviewed the ſcenes of the day
that was now nearly paſſed, with a
mixture of aſtoniſhment and diſtreſs, to
which no deſcription can be equal.
The ſudden and amazing change that
a few hours had made in his ſituation,
appeared like a wild and diſtreſsful
dream, from which he almoſt doubted
whether he ſhould not wake to the
power and the felicity that he had loſt.
He ſat ſome time bewildered in the
hurry and multiplicity of his thoughts,
and at length burſt out into paſſionate
exclamations :

exclamations: ' What,' fays he, ' and
' where am I ? Am I, indeed, HA-
' MET; that fon of Solyman who di-
' vided the dominion of Perfia with
' his brother, and who poffeffed the
' love of ALMEIDA alone ? Dreadful
' viciffitude! I am now an outcaft,
' friendlefs and forlorn; without an af-
' fociate, and without a dwelling: for
' me the cup of adverfity overflows,
' and the laft dregs of forrow have
' been wrung out for my portion : the
' powers not only of the earth, but
' of the air, have combined againft
' me ; and how can I ftand alone be-
' fore them ? But is there no power
' that will interpofe in my behalf ? If
' He, who is fupreme, is good, I fhall
' not perifh. But wherefore am I thus ?
' Why fhould the defires of vice be
                              ' accomplifhed

' accomplished by superior powers;
' and why should superior powers be
' permitted to disappoint the expecta-
' tions of virtue? Yet let me not
' rashly question the ways of Him, in
' whose balance the world is weighed:
' by Him, every evil is rendered sub-
' servient to good; and by His wisdom,
' the happiness of the whole is secured.
' Yet I am but a part only, and for a
' part only I can feel. To me, what
' is that goodness of which I do
' not partake? In my cup the gall is
' unmixed; and have I not, therefore,
' a right to complain? But what have
' I said? Let not the gloom that sur-
' rounds me, hide from me the pros-
' pect of immortality. Shall not eter-
' nity atone for time? Eternity, to
' which the duration of ages is but

' as

' as an atom to a world! Shall I not,
' when this momentary feparation is
' paft, again meet ALMEIDA to part
' no more? and fhall not a purer flame
' than burns upon the earth, unite us?
' Even at this moment, her mind, which
' not the frauds of forcery can taint or
' alienate, is mine: that pleafure which
' fhe referved for me, cannot be taken
' by force; it is in the confent alone
' that it fubfifts; and from the joy
' that fhe feels, and from that only,
' proceeds the joy fhe can beftow.'

With thefe reflections he foothed the
anguifh of his mind, till the dreadful
moment arrived, in which the power
of the talifman took place, and the figure of ALMORAN was changed into
' that

that of HAMET, and the figure of HA-
MET into that of ALMORAN.

At the moment of transformation,
HAMET was feized with a fudden lan-
guor, and his faculties were fufpended
as by the ftroke of death. When he
recovered, his limbs ftill trembled, and
his lips were parched with thirft : he
rofe, therefore, and entering the ca-
vern, at the mouth of which he had
been fitting, he ftooped over the well
to drink ; but glancing his eyes upon
the water, he faw, with aftonifhment
and horror, that it reflected, not his
own countenance, but that of his brother. He ftarted back from the prodigy ; and fupporting himfelf againft
the fide of the rock, he ftood fome
time like a ftatue, without the power
of

of recollection : but at length the thought suddenly rushed into his mind, that the same sorcery which had suspended his marriage, and driven him from the throne, was still practised against him; and that the change of his figure to that of ALMORAN, was the effect of ALMORAN's having assumed his likeness, to obtain, in this disguise, whatever ALMEIDA could bestow. This thought, like a whirlwind of the desert, totally subverted his mind; his fortitude was borne down, and his hopes were rooted up ; no principles remained to regulate his conduct, but all was phrenfy, confusion, and despair. He rushed out of the cave with a furious and distracted look ; and went in haste towards the city, without having formed any design, fign, or confidered any confequence that might follow.

The fhadows of the mountains were now lengthened by the declining fun; and the approach of evening had invited OMAR to meditate in a grove, that was adjacent to the gardens of the palace. From this place he was feen at fome diftance by HAMET, who came up to him with a hafty and difordered pace; and OMAR drew back with a cold and diftant reverence, which the power and the character of ALMORAN concurred to excite. HAMET, not reflecting upon the caufe of this behaviour, was offended, and reproached him with the want of that friendfhip he had fo often profeffed: the vehemence of his expreffion and demeanor, fuited well with

the

the appearance of ALMORAN; and
OMAR, as the beſt proof of that friend‑
ſhip which had been impeached, took
this opportunity to repeat his admoni-
tions in the behalf of HAMET : ' What
' ever evil,' ſaid he, ' thou canſt bring
' upon HAMET, will be doubled to
' thyſelf: to his virtues, the Power
' that fills infinitude is a friend, and he
' can be afflicted only till they are per-
' fect; but thy ſufferings will be the
' puniſhment of vice, and as long as
' thou art vicious they muſt increaſe.

HAMET, who inſtantly recollected
for whom he was miſtaken, and the
anguiſh of whoſe mind was for a moment ſuſpended by this teſtimony of
eſteem and kindneſs, which could not
poſſibly be feigned, and which was
paid

paid him at the rifque of life, when it
could not be known that he received
it; ran forward to embrace the hoary
fage, who had been the guide of his
youth, and cried out, in a voice that
was broken by contending paffions,
' The face is the face of ALMORAN;
' but the heart is the heart of HAMET.'

OMAR was ftruck dumb with aftonifhment; and HAMET, who was impatient to be longer miftaken, related all
the circumftances of his transformation, and reminded him of fome parti-
culars which could be known only to
themfelves : ' Canft thou not yet be-
' lieve,' faid he, ' that I am HAMET?
' when thou haft this day feen me
' banifhed from my kingdom; when
' thou haft now met me a fugitive

' returning from the defert; and when
' I learnt from thee, fince the fun
' was rifen which is not yet fet,
' that more than mortal powers were
' combined againft me.' ' I now
' believe,' faid OMAR, ' that thou,
' indeed, art HAMET.' ' Stay me not
' then,' faid HAMET; ' but come with
' me to revenge.' ' Beware,' faid O-
MAR, ' left thou endanger the lofs of
' more than empire and ALMEIDA.'
' If not to revenge,' faid HAMET,' I
' may at leaft be permitted to punifh.'
' Thy mind,' fays OMAR, ' is now in
' fuch a ftate, that to punifh the crimes
' by which thou haft been wronged,
' will dip thee in the guilt of blood.
' Why elfe are we forbidden to take
' vengeance for ourfelves ? and why is
' it referved as the prerogative of the
Moft

' Moſt High? In Him, and in Him
' alone, it is goodneſs guided by wiſ-
' dom : He approves the means, only
' as neceſſary to the end; He wounds
' only to heal, and deſtroys only to
' ſave; He has complacence, not in
' the evil, but in the good only
' which it is appointed to produce.
' Remember, therefore, that he, to
' whom the puniſhment of another
' is ſweet; though his act may be
' juſt with reſpect to others, with re-
' ſpect to himſelf it is a deed of
' darkneſs, and abhorred by the Al-
' mighty.' HAMET, who had ſtood
abſtracted in the contemplation of
the new injury he had ſuffered,
while OMAR was perſuading him not
to revenge it, ſtarted from his poſture in all the wildneſs of diſtrac-

tion;

' tion; and burſting away from OMAR,
' with an ardent and furious look
' haſted toward the palace, and was
' ſoon out of ſight.

CHAP.

CHAP. XV.

IN the mean time, ALMORAN, after having effected the transformation, was met, as he was going to the apartment of ALMEIDA, by Ofmyn. Ofmyn had already experienced the mifery of dependent greatnefs, that kept him continually under the eye of a capricious tyrant, whofe temper was various as the gales of fummer, and whofe anger was fudden as the bolt of heaven; whofe purpofe and paffions were dark and impetuous as the midnight ftorm, and at whofe command death was inevitable as the approach of time. When

E 3   he

he saw ALMORAN, therefore, in the likeness of HAMET, he felt a secret desire to apprize him of his situation, and offer him his friendship.

ALMORAN, who with the form assumed the manners of HAMET, addressed Osmyn with a mild though mournful countenance: ' At length,' said he, ' the will of ALMORAN alone ' is law; does it permit me to hold a ' private rank in this place, without ' molestation? It permits,' said Osmyn, ' yet more; he has commanded, that ' you should have admittance to AL-' MEIDA.' ALMORAN, whose vanity betrayed him to flatter his own power in the person of HAMET, replied with a smile: ' I know, that ALMO-' RAN, who presides like a God in si-

lent

' lent and diftant ftate, reveals the fe-
' crets of his will to thee; I know
' that thou art'—' I am,' faid Ofmyn,
' of all thou feeft, moft wretch-
' ed.' At this declaration, ALMORAN
turned fhort, and fixed his eyes upon
Ofmyn with a look of furprize and anger : ' Does not the favour of ALMO-
' RAN,' faid he, ' whofe fmile is pow-
' er, and wealth, and honour, fhine
' upon thee?' ' My lord,' faid Ofmyn, ' I know fo well the feverity of
' thy virtue, that if I fhould, even for
' thy fake, become perfidious to thy
' brother'—— ALMORAN, who was
unable to preferve the character of
HAMET with propriety, interrupted
him with a fierce and haughty tone :
' How !' faid he, ' perfidious to

my

' my brother ! to ALMORAN perfidi-
' ous !

Ofmyn, who had now gone too far
to recede, and who ftill faw before
him the figure of HAMET, proceeded
in his purpofe: ' I knew,' faid he,
' that in thy judgment I fhould be
' condemned; and yet, the preferva-
' tion of life is the ftrongeft principle
' of nature, and the love of virtue is
' her proudeft boaft.' ' Explain thy-
' felf,' faid ALMORAN, ' for I cannot
' comprehend thee.' ' I mean,' faid
Ofmyn, ' that he, whofe life depends
' upon the caprice of a tyrant, is like
' the wretch whofe fentence is already
' pronounced; and who, if the wind
' does but rufh by his dungeon, ima-
' gines that it is the bow-ftring and the
' mute.

' mute.' ' Fear not,' said Almoran, who now affected to be again
calm; ' be ftill faithful, and thou
' fhalt ftill be fafe.' ' Alas!' said Ofmyn, ' there is no diligence, no toil,
' no faith, that can fecure the flave
' from the fudden phrenfy of paffion,
' from the caufelefs rage either of
' drunkennefs or luft. I am that flave;
' the flave of a tyrant whom I hate.'
The confufion of Almoran was now
too great to be concealed, and he ftood
filent with rage, fear, and indignation.
Ofmyn, fuppofing that his wonder fufpended his belief of what he had
heard, confirmed his declaration by an
oath.

Whoever thou art, to whofe mind
Almoran, the mighty and the proud,

is

is prefent; before whom, the lord of
abfolute dominion ftands trembling and
rebuked; who feeft the poffeffor of
power by which nature is controuled,
pale and filent with anguifh and difappointment: if, in the fury of thy wrath,
thou haft aggravated weaknefs into
guilt; if thou haft chilled the glow of
affection, when it fluſhed the cheek in
thy prefence, with the frown of difpleafure, or repreffed the ardour of friendfhip with indifference or neglect ; now,
let thy heart fmite thee : for, in thy
folly, thou haft caft away that gem,
which is the light of life ; which power
can never feize, and which gold can
never buy !

The tyrant fell at once from his
pride, like a ftar from Heaven ; and
Ofmyn,

Ofmyn, ftill addreffing him as HA-
MET, at once increafed his mifery and
his fears : ' O,' faid he, ' that the
' throne of Perfia was thine ! then
' fhould innocence enjoy her birth-right
'· of peace, and hope fhould bid honeft
' induftry look upward. There is not
' one to whom ALMORAN has delegat-
' ed· power, nor one on whom his
' tranfient favour has beftowed any
' gift, who does not already feel his
'· heart throb with the pangs of boding
' terror. Nor is there one who, if he
' did not fear the difpleafure of the in-
' vifible power by whom the throne
' has been given to thy brother, would
' not immediately revolt to thee.'

ALMORAN, who had hitherto remained filent, now burft into a paffio-
2   nate

nate exclamation of felf pity: 'What
'can I do?' faid he; 'and whither
'can I turn?' Ofmyn, who miftook
the caufe of his diftrefs, and fuppofed
that he deplored only his want of
power to avail himfelf of the general
difpofition in his favour, endeavoured to fortify his mind againft
defpair: 'Your ftate,' faid he, 'in-
'deed is diftrefsful, but not hopelefs.'
The king who, though addreffed as
HAMET, was ftill betrayed by his confufion to anfwer as ALMORAN, fmote
his breaft, and replied in an agony,
'It is hopelefs!' Ofmyn remarked
his emotion and defpair, with a concern and aftonifhment that ALMORAN
obferved, and at once recollected his
fituation. He endeavoured to retract
fuch expreffions of trouble and def-
pondency,

pondency, as did not fuit the character
he had aſſumed; and telling Oſmyn,
that he thanked him for his friendſhip,
and would improve the advantages it
offered him, he directed him to acquaint the eunuchs that they were to
admit him to ALMEIDA. When he
was left alone, his doubts and perplex-
ity held him long in fuſpenſe; a thou-
ſand expedients occurred to his mind
by turns, and by turns were rejected.

His firſt thought was to put Oſmyn
to death: but he conſidered, that by
this he would gain no advantage, as
he would be in equal danger from whoever ſhould ſucceed him: he conſidered alſo, that againſt Oſmyn he was
upon his guard; and that he might at
any time learn, from him, whatever
deſign

defign might be formed in favour of
HAMET, by affuming HAMET's appearance: that he would thus be the
confident of every fecret, in which his
own fafety was concerned; and might
difconcert the beft contrived project at
the very moment of its execution,
when it would be too late for other
meafures to be taken: he determined,
therefore, to let Ofmyn live; at leaft,
till it became more neceffary to cut
him off. Having in fome degree
foothed and fortified his mind by
thefe reflections, he entered the apartment of ALMEIDA.

His hope was not founded upon a
defign to marry her under the appearance of HAMET; for that would be impoffible, as the ceremony muft have
been performed by the priefts who fup-

poted

pofed the marriage with HAMET to have been forbidden by a divine command; and who, therefore, would not have confented, even fuppofing they would otherwife have ventured, at the requeft of HAMET, to perform a ceremony which they knew would be difpleafing to ALMORAN: but he hoped to take advantage of her tendernefs for his brother, and the particular circumftances of her fituation, which made the folemnities of marriage impoffible, to feduce her to gratify his defires, without the fanction which alone rendered the gratification of them lawful: if he fucceeded in this defign, he had reafon to expect, either that his love would be extinguifhed by enjoyment; or that, if he fhould ftill defire to marry ALMEIDA, he might, by difclofing to her the artifice by which he had

effected

effected his purpofe, prevail upon her to confent, as her connexion with HA-MET, the chief obftacle to her marriage with him, would then be broken for ever; and as fhe might, perhaps, wifh to fanctify the pleafure which fhe might be not unwilling to repeat, or at leaft to make that lawful which it would not be in her power to prevent.

In this difpofition, and with this de-fign, he was admitted to ALMEIDA; who, without fufpicion of her danger, was expofed to the fevereft trial, in which every paffion concurred to oppofe her virtue: fhe was folicited by all the powers of fubtilty and defire, under the appearance of a lover whofe ten-dernefs and fidelity had been long tried, and whofe paffion fhe returned with equal

equal conftancy and ardour; and fhe was thus folicited, when the rites which alone could confecrate their union, were impoffible, and were rendered impoffible by the guilty defigns of a rival, in whofe power fhe was, and from whom no other expedient offered her a deliverance. Thus deceived and betrayed, fhe received him with an excefs of tendernefs and joy, which flattered all his hopes, and for a moment fufpended his mifery. She enquired, with a fond and gentle folicitude, by what means he had gained admittance, and how he had provided for his retreat. He received and returned her careffes with a vehemence, in which, to lefs partial eyes, defire would have been more apparent than love; and in the tumult of his paffion, he almoft neglected her

enquiries : finding, however, that fhe
would be anfwered, he told her, that
being by the permiffion of ALMORAN
admitted to every part of the palace,
except that of the women, he had
found means to bribe the eunuch who
kept the door; who was not in danger
of detection, becaufe ALMORAN, wea-
ried with the tumult and fatigue of
the day, had retired to fleep, and
given order to be called at a certain
hour. She then complained of the fo-
licitations to which fhe was expofed,
expreffed her dread of the confequences
fhe had reafon to expect from fome fudden fally of the tyrant's rage, and related with tears the brutal outrage
fhe had fuffered when he laft left her:
‘ Though I abhorred him,’ faid fhe,
‘ I yet kneeled before him for thee.
‘ Let

' Let me bend in reverence to that
' Power, at whose look the whirlwinds
' are silent, and the seas are calm, that
' his fury has hitherto been restrained
' from hurting thee!'

At these words, the face of ALMO-
RAN was again covered with the blushes
of confusion : to be still beloved only
as HAMET, and as ALMORAN to be
still hated ; to be thus reproached without anger, and wounded by those who
knew not that they struck him ; was a
species of misery peculiar to himself,
and had been incurred only by the ac-
quisition of new powers, which he had
requested and received as necessary to
obtain that felicity, which the parsi-
mony of nature had placed beyond his
reach. His emotions, however, as by

ALMEIDA

ALMEIDA they were suppofed to be the emotions of HAMET, she imputed to a different caufe : ' As Heaven,' fays she, ' has preferved thee from ' death ; fo has it, for thy fake, pre-' ' ferved me from violation.' ALMO-RAN, whofe paffion had in this interval again furmounted his remorfe, gazed eagerly upon her, and catching her to his bofom ; ' Let us at leaft,' fays he, ' fecure the happinefs that is now of-' fered ; let not thefe ineftimable mo-' ments pafs by us unimproved ; but ' to shew that we deferve them, let ' them be devoted to love.' ' Let us ' then,' faid ALMEIDA, ' efcape toge-' ther.' ' To efcape with thee,' faid ALMORAN, ' is impoffible. I shall re-' tire, and, like the shaft of Arabia, ' leave no mark behind me ; but the

' flight

' flight of ALMEIDA will at once be
' traced to him by whom I was ad-
' mitted, and I fhall thus retaliate his
' friendfhip with deftruction.' ' Let
' him then,' faid ALMEIDA, ' be the
' partner of our flight.' ' Urge it not
' now,' faid ALMORAN ; ' but truft to
' my prudence and my love, to felect
' fome hour that will be more favour-
' able to our purpofe. And yet,' faid
he, ' even then, we fhall, as now,
' figh in vain for the completion of
' our wifhes : by whom fhall our hands
' be joined, when in the opinion of
' the priefts it has been forbidden from
' above?' ' Save thyfelf then,' faid AL-
MEIDA, ' and leave me to my fate.'
' Not fo,' faid ALMORAN. ' What
' elfe,' replied ALMEIDA, ' is in our
' power ?' ' It is in our power,' faid

ALMORAN, ' to feize that joy, to which
' a public form can give us no new
' claim ; for the public form can only
' declare that right by which I claim
' it now.'

As they were now reclining upon a
fofa, he threw his arm round her; but
fhe fuddenly fprung up, and burft from
him : the tear ftarted to her eye, and
fhe gazed upon him with an earneft but
yet tender look : ' Is it ?' fays fhe—' No
' fure, it is not the voice of HAMET !'
' O ! yes,' faid ALMORAN, ' what
' other voice fhould call thee to cancel
' at once the wrongs of HAMET and
' ALMEIDA ; to fecure the treafures of
' thy love from the hand of the rob-
' ber ; to hide the joys, which if now
' we lofe we may lofe for ever, in the
' facred

' facred and inviolable ftores of the paft,
' and place them beyond the power
' not of ALMORAN only but of fate?'
With this wild effufion of defire, he
caught her again to his breaft, and
finding no refiftance his heart exulted
in his fuccefs; but the next moment,
to the total difappointment of his hopes,
he perceived that fhe had fainted in his
arms. When fhe recovered, fhe once
more difengaged herfelf from him, and
turning away her face, fhe burft into
tears. When her voice could be heard,
fhe covered herfelf with her veil, and
turning again towards him, ' All but
' this,' faid fhe, ' I had learnt to bear;
' and how has this been deferved by AL-
' MEIDA of HAMET? You was my only
' folace in diftrefs; and when the tears
' have ftolen from my eyes in filence

F 4 ' and

' and in folitude, I thought on thee; I'
' thought upon the chafte ardour of
' thy facred friendfhip, which was
' foftened, refined, and exalted into
' love. This was my hoarded treafure;
' and the thoughts of poffeffing this,
' foothed all my anguifh with a mifer's
' happinefs, who, bleft in the confci-
' oufnefs of hidden wealth, defpifes
' cold and hunger, and rejoices in the
' midft of all the miferies that make
' poverty dreadful: this was my laft
' retreat; but I am now defolate and
' forlorn, and my foul looks round,
' with terror, for that refuge which it
' can never find.' ' Find that refuge,'
faid ALMORAN, ' in me.' ' Alas!'
faid ALMEIDA, ' can he afford me re-
' fuge from my forrows, who, for the
' guilty pleafures of a tranfient mo-
' ment,

' ment, would for ever fully the purity
' of my mind, and aggravate misfor-
' tune by the confcioufnefs of guilt ?'

As ALMORAN now perceived, that
it was impoffible, by any importunity,
to induce her to violate her principles;
he had nothing more to attempt, but
to fubvert them. ' When,' faid he,
' fhall ALMEIDA awake, and thefe
' dreams of folly and fuperftition va-
' nifh ? That only is virtue, by which
' happinefs is produced; and whatever
' produces happinefs, is therefore vir-
' tue; and the forms, and words, and
' rites, which priefts have pretended to
' be required by Heaven, are the
' fraudful arts only by which they go-
' vern mankind.'

ALMEIDA,

ALMEIDA, by this impious infult, was roufed from grief to indignation : ' As thou haft now dared,' faid fhe, ' to deride the laws, which thou ' wouldft firft have broken ; fo haft ' thou broken for ever the tender ' bonds, by which my foul was united ' to thine. Such as I fondly believed ' thee, thou art not; and what thou ' art, I have never loved. I have ' loved a delufive phantom only, which, ' while I ftrove to grafp it, has va- ' nifhed from me.' ALMORAN attempt- ed to reply ; but on fuch a fubject, neither her virtue nor her wifdom would permit debate. ' That prodigy,' faid fhe, ' which I thought was the ' fleight of cunning, or the work of ' forcery, I now revere as the voice of ' Heaven; which, as it knew thy heart,

' has

' has in mercy faved me from thy
' arms. To the will of Heaven fhall
' my will be obedient; and my voice
' alfo fhall pronounce, to Almoran
' Almeida.'

Almoran, whofe whole foul was now
fufpended in attention, conceived new
hopes of fuccefs; and forefaw the certain accomplifhment of his purpofe,
though by an effect directly contrary
to that which he had laboured to produce. Thus to have incurred the hatred of Almeida in the form of Hamet, was more fortunate than to have
taken advantage of her love; the path
that led to his wifhes was now clear
and open; and his marriage with Almeida in his own perfon, waited only
till he could refume it. He, therefore,

inftead

inftead of foothing, provoked her refentment : ' If thou haft loved a phan-
' tom,' faid he, ' which exifted only in
' imagination ; on fuch a phantom my
' love alfo has been fixed : thou haft,
' indeed, only the form of what I
' called ALMEIDA ; my love thou haft
' rejected, becaufe thou haft never
' loved ; the object of thy paffion was
' not HAMET, but a throne ; and thou
' haft made the obfervance of rituals,
' in which folly only can fuppofe there
' is good or ill, a pretence to violate
' thy faith, that thou mayft ftill gra-
' tify thy ambition.'

To this injurious reproach, ALMEI-
DA made no reply; and ALMORAN
immediately quitted her apartment,
that he might reaffume his own figure,
and

and take advantage of the difpofition which, under the appearance of HA-MET, he had produced in favour of himfelf: But Ofmyn, who fuppofing him to be HAMET, had intercepted and detained him as he was going to ALMEI-DA, now intercepted him a fecond time at his return, having placed himfelf near the door of the apartment for that purpofe.

Ofmyn was by no means fatisfied with the iffue of their laft interview : he had perceived a perturbation in the mind of ALMORAN, for which, imagining him to be HAMET, he could not account ; and which feemed more extra-ordinary upon a review, than when it happened ; he, therefore, again entered into converfation with him, in which he
farther

6

farther difclofed his fentiments and defigns. ALMORAN, notwithftanding
the impatience natural to his temper
and fituation, was thus long detained
liftening to Ofmyn, by the united influence of his curiofity and his fears;
his enquiries ftill alarmed him with new
terrors, by difcovering new objects of
diftruft, and new inftances of difaffec-
tion: ftill, however, he refolved, not
yet to remove Ofmyn from his poft,
that he might give no alarm by any
appearance of fufpicion, and confequently learn with more eafe, and detect with more certainty, any project
that might be formed againft him.

C H A P.

C H A P. XVI.

ALMEIDA, as foon as fhe was left alone, began to review the fcene that had juft paft; and was every moment affected with new wonder, grief, and refentment. She now deplored her own misfortune; and now conceived a defign to punifh the author of it, from whofe face fhe fuppofed the hand of adverfity had torn the mafk under which he had deceived her: it appeared to her very eafy, to take a fevere revenge upon HAMET for the indignity which fhe fuppofed he had offered her, by complaining of it

to

to ALMORAN; and telling him, that he had gained admittance to her by bribing the eunuch who kept the door. The thought of thus giving him up, was one moment rejected, as arising from a vindictive spirit; and the next indulged, as an act of justice to ALMORAN, and a punishment due to the hypocrify of HAMET: to the firft she inclined, when her grief, which was still mingled with a tender remembrance of the man she loved, was predominant; and to the laft, when her grief gave way to indignation.

Thus are we inclined to confider the fame action, either as a virtue, or a vice, by the influence of different paffions, which prompt us either to perform or to avoid it. ALMEIDA, from deliberating

liberating whether fhe fhould accufe
HAMET to ALMORAN, or conceal his
fault, was led to confider what punifhment he would either incur or efcape
in confequence, of her determination;
and the images that rufhed into her
mind, the moment this became the object of her thoughts, at once determined her to be filent: ' Could I bear
' to fee,' faid fhe, ' that hand, which
' has fo often trembled with delight
' when it enfolded mine, convulfed
' and black! thofe eyes, that as often
' as they gazed upon me were diffolv-
' ed in tears of tendernefs and love,
' ftart from the fockets! and thofe lips
' that breathed the fofteft fighs of ele-
' gant defire, diftorted and gafping in
' the convulfions of death!'

From this image, her mind recoiled in an agony of terror and pity; her heart funk within her; her limbs trembled; fhe funk down upon the fofa, and burft into tears.

By this time, HAMET, on whofe form the likenefs of ALMORAN was ftill impreffed, had reached the palace. He went inftantly towards the apartment of the women. Inftead of that chearful alacrity, that mixture of zeal and reverence and affeƈtion, which his eye had been ufed to find wherever it was turned, he now obferved confufion, anxiety and terror; whoever he met, made hafte to proftrate themfelves before him, and feared to look up till he was paft. He went on, however, with a hafty pace; and coming up to to the eunuch's guard, he faid with an impatient tone ; ' To ALMEIDA.' The flave immediately made way before him, and conducted him to the door of the apartment, which he would not otherwife have been able to find, and for which he could not directly enquire.

When he entered, his countenance expreffed all the paffions that his fituation had roufed in his mind. He firft looked fternly round him, to fee whether ALMORAN was not prefent ; and then fetching a deep figh he turned his eyes, with a look of mournful tendernefs, upon ALMEIDA. His firft view was to difcover, whether ALMORAN had already fupplanted him ; and for this purpofe he collected the whole ftrength

G 2 of

of his mind : he confidered that he appeared now, not as HAMET, but as ALMORAN; and that he was to queftion ALMEIDA concerning ALMORAN, while fhe had miftaken him for HAMET ; he was therefore to maintain the character, at whatever expence, till his doubts were refolved, and his fears either removed or confirmed : he was fo firmly perfuaded, that ALMORAN had been there before him, that he did not afk the queftion, but fuppofed the fact ; he reftrained alike both his tendernefs and his fears; and looking earneftly upon ALMEIDA, who had rifen up in his prefence with blufhes and confufion, ' To me,' fays he, ' is ' ALMEIDA ftill cold ? and has fhe la- ' vifhed all her love upon HAMET ?'

At

At the name of HAMET, the blushes and confusion of ALMEIDA increased: her mind was still full of the images, which had risen from the thought of what HAMET might suffer, if ALMORAN should know that he had been with her; and though she feared that their interview was discovered, yet she hoped it might be only suspected, and in that case the removal or confirmation of the suspicions, on which the fate of HAMET depended, would devolve upon her.

In this situation, she, who had but a few moments before doubted, whether she should not voluntarily give him up, when nothing more was necessary for his safety than to be silent; now determined, with whatever reluc-

tance,

tance, to fecure him, though it could not be done without diffimulation, and though it was probable that in this diffimulation fhe would be detected. Inftead, therefore, of anfwering the queftion, fhe repeated it: ' On whom ' faid my lord, on HAMET?' HAMET, whofe fufpicions were increafed by the evafion, replied with great emotion, ' Aye, on HAMET; did he not this ' moment leave you?' ' Leave me this ' moment?' faid ALMEIDA, with yet greater confufion, and deeper blufhes. HAMET, in the impatience of his jea-loufy, concluded, that the paffions which he faw expreffed in her counte-nance, and which arofe from the ftrug-gle between her regard to truth and her tendernefs for HAMET, proceeded

from

from the confcioufnefs of what he had
moft reafon to dread, and fhe to conceal, a breach of virtue, to which fhe
had been betrayed by his own appearance united with the vices of his
brother: he, therefore, drew back from
her with a look of inexpreffible anguifh, and ftood fome time filent. She
obferved, that in his countenance there
was more expreffion of trouble, than
rage; fhe, therefore, hoped to divert
him from perfuing his enquiries, by
at once removing his jealoufy; which
fhe fuppofed would be at an end, as
foon as fhe fhould difclofe the refolution
fhe had taken in his favour. Addreffing him, therefore, as ALMORAN, with
a voice which though it was gentle and
foothing, was yet mournful and tremu-
lous; ' Do not turn from me,' faid fhe,

' with

‘ with thofe unfriendly and frowning
‘ looks; give me now that love which
‘ fo lately you offered, and with all the
‘ future I will atone the paft.’

Upon HAMET, whofe heart involuntarily anfwered to the voice of AL-
MEIDA, thefe words had irrefiftible and
inftantaneous force; but recollecting,
in a moment, whofe form he bore, and
to whom they were addreffed, they
ftruck him with new aftonifhment, and
increafed the torments of his mind.
Suppofing what he at firft feared had
happened, and that ALMORAN had feduced her as HAMET; he could not account for her now addreffing him, as
ALMORAN, with words of favour and
compliance: he, therefore, renewed his
enquiries concerning himfelf, with apprehenfions

prehenfions of a different kind. She, who was ftill folicitous to put an end to the enquiry, as well for the fake of HAMET, as to prevent her own embarraffment, replied with a figh, ‘ Let ‘ not thy peace be interrupted by one ‘ thought of HAMET ; for of HAMET ‘ ALMEIDA fhall think no more.’ HAMET, who, though he had fortified himfelf againft whatever might have happened to her perfon, could not bear the alienation of her mind, cried out, with looks of diftraction and a voice fcarcely human, ‘ Not think of ‘ HAMET !’ ALMEIDA, whofe aftonifhment was every moment increafing, replied, with a tender and interefting enquiry, ‘ Is ALMORAN then offended, ‘ that AIMEIDA fhould think of HA ‘ MET no more ?’ HAMET, being thus

addreffed

addreffed by the name of his brother,
again recollected his fituation; and now
firft conceived the idea, that the alte-
ration of ALMEIDA's fentiments with
refpect to himfelf, might be the effect
of fome violence offered her by ALMO-
RAN in his likenefs; he, therefore, re-
curred to his firft purpofe, and determined, by a direct enquiry, to difcover, whether fhe had feen him under
that appearance. This enquiry he
urged with the utmoft folemnity and
ardour, in terms fuitable to his prefent
appearance and fituation: ' Tell me,'
faid he, ' have thefe doors been open
' to HAMET ? Has he obtained poffef-
' fion of that treafure, which, by the
' voice of Heaven, has been allotted to
' me ?'

To

To this double queftion, ALMEIDA anfwered by a fingle negative; and her anfwer, therefore, was both falfe and true: it was true that her perfon was ftill inviolate, and it was true alfo that HAMET had not been admitted to her; yet her denial of it was falfe, for fhe believed the contrary; ALMORAN only had been admitted, but fhe had received him as his brother. HAMET, however, was fatisfied with the anfwer, and did not difcover its fallacy. He looked up to Heaven, with an expreffion of gratitude and joy; and then turning to ALMEIDA, 'Swear then,' faid he, 'that thou haft granted to 'HAMET, no pledge of thy love which 'fhould be referved for me.' ALMEIDA, who now thought nothing more than the affeveration neceffary to quiet

his

his mind, immediately complied : ' I
' fwear,' faid fhe, ' that to Hamet
' I have given nothing, which thou
' wouldft wifh me to with-hold : the
' power that has devoted my perfon to
' thee, has difunited my heart from
' Hamet, whom I renounce in thy
' prefence for ever.'

Hamet, whofe fortitude and recollection were again overborne, was
thrown into an agitation of mind,
which difcovered itfelf by looks and
geftures very different from thofe which
Almeida had expected, and overwhelmed her with new confufion and
difappointment : that he, who had fo
lately folicited her love with all the vehemence of a defire impatient to be
gratified, fhould now receive a declaration

ration that fhe was ready to comply,
with marks of diftrefs and anger, was
a myftery which fhe could not folve. In
the mean time, the ftruggle in his breaft
became every moment more violent:
' Where then,' faid he, ' is the con-
' ftancy which you vowed to HAMET ;
' and for what inftance of his love is
' he now forfaken ?'

ALMEIDA was now more embarraf-
fed than before ; fhe felt all the force of
the reproof, fuppofing it to have been
given by ALMORAN ; and fhe could be
juftified only by relating the particular,
which at the expence of her fincerity
fhe had determined to conceal. AL-
MORAN was now exalted in her opinion, while his form was animated by
the fpirit of HAMET; as much as

HAMET

HAMET had been degraded, while his form was animated by the fpirit of ALMORAN. In his refentment of her perfidy to his rival, though it favoured his fondeft and moft ardent wifhes, there was an abhorrence of vice, and a ge-nerofity of mind, which fhe fuppofed to have been incompatible with his chara&ter. To his reproach, fhe could reply only by complaint; and could no otherwife evade his queftion, than by obferving the inconfiftency of his own behaviour: ' Your words,' faid fhe, ' are daggers to my heart. You ' condemn me for a compliance with ' your own wifhes; and for obedience ' to that voice, which you fuppofed to ' have revealed the will of Heaven. Has ' the caprice of defire already wander-' ed to a new obje&? and do you

' now feek a pretence to refufe, when
' it is freely offered, what fo lately you
' would have taken by force ?'.

HAMET, who was now fired with refentment againft ALMEIDA, whom yet
he could not behold without defire;
and who, at the fame moment, was
impatient to revenge his wrongs upon
ALMORAN; was fuddenly prompted
to fatisfy all his paffions, by taking advantage of the wiles of ALMORAN,
and the perfidy of ALMEIDA, to defeat
the one and to punifh the other. It
was now in his power inftantly to con-
fummate his marriage, as a prieft might
be procured without a moment's delay,
and as ALMEIDA's confent was already
given; he would then obtain the poffeffion of her perfon, by the very act

in

in which she perfidiously refigned it to his rival ; to whom he would then leave the beauties he had already poffeffed, and caft from him in difdain, as united with a mind that he could never love. As his imagination was fired with the firft conception of this defign, he caught her to his breaft with a fury, in which all the paffions in all their rage were at once concentered : ' Let ' the prieft,' faid he, ' inftantly unite ' us. Let us comprize, in one mo- ' ment, in this inftant, now, our whole ' of being, and exclude alike the fu- ' ture and the paft !' Then grafping her ftill in his arms, he looked up to heaven : ' Ye powers,' faid he, ' in- ' vifible but yet prefent, who mould ' my changing and unrefifting form ; ' prolong, but for one hour, that

' myfterious

' myfterious charm, that is now upon
' me, and I will be ever after fubfer-
' vient to your will!'

ALMEIDA, who was terrified at the
furious ardor of this unintelligible addrefs, fhrunk from his embrace, pale
and trembling, without power to reply. HAMET gazed tenderly upon
her; and recollecting the purity and
tendernefs with which he had loved
her, his virtues fuddenly recovered their
force; he difmiffed her from his embrace; and turning from her, he
dropped in filence the tear that ftarted
to his eye, and expreffed, in a low and
faultering voice, the thoughts that rufhed upon his mind: ' No,' faid he;
' HAMET fhall ftill difdain the joy,
' which is at once fordid and tranfient:

VOL. II. H ' in

' in the breaſt of HAMET, luſt ſhall
' not be the pander of revenge. Shall
' I, who have languiſhed for the pure
' delight which can ariſe only from
' the interchange of ſoul with ſoul,
' and is endeared by mutual confi-
' dence and complacency; ſhall I ſnatch
' under this diſguiſe, which belies my
' features and degrades my virtue, a
' caſual poſſeſſion of faithleſs beauty,
' which I deſpiſe and hate? Let this
' be the portion of thoſe, that hate
' me without a cauſe; but let this be
' far from me!' At this thought, he
felt a ſudden elation of mind; and the
conſcious dignity of virtue, that in
ſuch a conflict was victorious, rendered him, in this glorious moment, ſuperior to miſfortune: his geſture became
calm, and his countenance ſedate; he

conſidered

confidered the wrongs he fuffered, not as a fufferer, but as a judge; and he determined at once to difcover himfelf to ALMEIDA, and to reproach her with her crime. He remarked her confu-fion without pity, as the effect not of grief but of guilt; and fixing his eyes upon her, with the calm feverity of a fuperior and offended being, ' Such,' faid he, ' is the benevolence of the ' Almighty to the children of the duft, ' that our misfortunes are, like poi- ' fons, antidotes to each other.'

ALMEIDA, whofe faculties were now fufpended by wonder and expectation, looked earneftly at him, but continued filent. ' Thy looks,' faid HAMET, ' are full of wonder; but as yet thy ' wonder has no caufe, in comparifon

' of

' of that which fhall be revealed. Thou
' knoweft the prodigy, which fo lately
' parted Hamet and Almeida: I am
' that Hamet, thou art that Almei-
' da.' Almeida would now have interrupted him; but Hamet raifed his
voice, and demanded to be heard: ' At
' that moment,' faid he, ' wretched
' as I am, the child of error and dif-
' obedience, my heart repined in fecret
' at the deftiny which had been written
' upon my head; for I then thought
' thee faithful and conftant: but if
' our hands had been then united, I
' fhould have been more wretched than
' I am; for I now know that thou
' art fickle and falfe. To know thee,
' though it has pierced my foul with
' forrow, has yet healed the wound
' which was inflicted when I loft thee:
' and

' and though I am now compelled to
' wear the form of ALMORAN, whofe
' vices are this moment difgracing mine,
' yet in the balance I fhall be weighed
' as HAMET, and I fhall fuffer only as
' I am found wanting.'

ALMEIDA, whofe mind was now in
a tumult that bordered upon diftraction, bewildered in a labyrinth of doubt
and wonder, and alike dreading the
confequence of what fhe heard, whether it was falfe or true, was yet impatient to confute or confirm it; and as
foon as fhe had recovered her fpeech,
urged him for fome token of the prodigy he afferted, which he might eafily
have given, by relating any of the in-
cidents which themfelves only could
know. But juft at this moment, AL-

H 3 MORAN,

MORAN, having at laſt diſengaged himſelf from Oſmyn, by whom he had
been long detained, reſumed his own
figure : and while the eyes of ALMEI-
DA were fixed upon HAMET, his powers
were ſuddenly taken from him, and reſtored in an inſtant; and ſhe beheld
the features of ALMORAN vaniſh, and
gazed with aſtoniſhment upon his own :
' Thy features change!' ſaid ſhe, ' and
' thou indeed art HAMET.' ' The ſud-
' den trance,' ſaid he, ' has reſtored
' me to myſelf; and from my wrongs
' where ſhalt thou be hidden ?' This
reproach was more than ſhe could ſuſ-
tain; but he caught her as ſhe was fal-
ling, and ſupported her in his arms.
This incident renewed in a moment all
the tenderneſs of his love : while he
beheld her diſtreſs, and preſſed her by
the

6

the embrace that fuſtained her to his boſom, he forgot every injury which he ſuppoſed ſhe had done him; and perceived her recover with a pleaſure, that for a moment fuſpended the ſenſe of his misfortunes.

Her firſt reflection was upon the ſnare, in which ſhe had been taken; and her firſt ſenſation was joy that ſhe had eſcaped: ſhe ſaw at once the whole complication of events that had deceived and diſtreſſed her; and nothing more was now neceſſary, than to explain them to HAMET; which, however, ſhe could not do, without diſcovering the inſincerity of her anſwers to the enquiries which he had made, while ſhe miſtook him for his brother: ' If ' in my heart,' ſays ſhe, ' thou haſt

' found

' found any virtue, let it incline thee
' to pity the vice that is mingled with
' it: by the vice I have been enfnared,
' but I have been delivered by the vir-
' tue. ALMORAN, for now I know
' that it was not thee, ALMORAN,
' when he poffeffed thy form, was with
' me: he prophaned thy love, by at-
' tempts to fupplant my virtue; I re-
' fifted his importunity, and efcaped
' perdition; but the guilt of ALMO-
' RAN drew my refentment upon HA-
' MET. I thought the vices which,
' under thy form, I difcovered in his
' bofom, were thine; and in the an-
' guifh of grief, indignation, and dif-
' appointment, my heart renounced
' thee: yet, as I could not give thee
' up to death, I could not difcover to
' ALMORAN the attempt which I im-
' puted

‘ puted to thee; when you queſtioned
‘ me, therefore, as ALMORAN, I was
‘ betrayed to diſſimulation, by the ten-
‘ derneſs which ſtill melted my heart
‘ for HAMET.’ ‘ I believe thee,’ ſaid
HAMET, catching her in a tranſport to
his breaſt : ‘ I love thee for thy vir-
‘ tue; and may the pure and exalted
‘ beings, who are ſuperior to the paſ-
‘ ſions that now throb in my heart,
‘ forgive me, if I love thee alſo for
‘ thy fault. Yet, let the danger to
‘ which it betrayed thee, teach us ſtill
‘ to walk in the ſtrait path, and com-
‘ mit the keeping of our peace to the
‘ Almighty; for he that wanders in
‘ the maze of falſehood, ſhall paſs by
‘ the good that he would meet, and
‘ ſhall meet the evil that he would ſhun.
‘ I alſo was tempted; but I was ſtrength-

5 ‘ ened

' ened to refift : if I had ufed the
' power, which I derived from the arts
' that have been practifed againft me,
' to return evil for evil ; if I had not
' difdained a fecret and unavowed re-
' venge, and the unhallowed pleafures
' of a brutal appetite ; I might have
' poffeffed thee in the form of ALMO-
' RAN, and have wronged irreparably
' myfelf and thee : for how could I
' have been admitted, as HAMET, to
' the beauties which I had enjoyed
' as ALMORAN ? and how couldft thou
' have given, to ALMORAN, what in
' reality had been appropriated by
' HAMET ?'

C H A P.

C H A P. XVII.

BUT while ALMEIDA and HAMET were thus congratulating each other upon the evils which they had efcaped, they were threatened by others, which, however obvious, they had overlooked.

ALMORAN, who was now exulting in the profpect of fuccefs that had exceeded his hopes, and who fuppofed the poffeffion of ALMEIDA before the end of the next hour, was as certain as that the next hour would arrive, fuddenly entered the apartment; but upon difcovering HAMET, he ftarted

back

back aftonifhed and difappointed. HA-
MET ftood unmoved; and regarded
him with a fixed and fteady look, that
at once reproached and confounded
him. ' What treachery,' faid ALMO-
RAN, ' has been practifed againft me?
' What has brought thee to this place;
' and how haft thou gained admit-
' tance?' ' Againft thy peace,' faid
HAMET, ' no treachery has been prac-
' tifed, but by thyfelf. By thofe arts
' in which thy vices have employed
' the powers of darknefs, I have been
' brought hither; and by thofe arts
' I have gained admittance: thy form
' which they have impofed upon me,
' was my paffport; and by the reftora-
' tion of my own, I have detected and
' difappointed the fraud, which the
' double change was produced to exe-
                              ' cute.

' cute. ALMEIDA, whom, as HA-
' MET, thou couldſt teach to hate thee,
' it is now impoſſible that, as ALMO-
' RAN, thou ſhouldſt teach to love.'

ALMEIDA, who perceived the ſtorm
to be gathering which the next moment would burſt upon the head of
HAMET, interpoſed between them, and
addreſſed each of them by turns ; urg-
ing HAMET to be ſilent, and conjuring
ALMORAN to be merciful. AL-
MORAN, however, without regarding
ALMEIDA, or making any reply to
HAMET, ſtruck the ground with his
foot, and the meſſengers of death, to
whom the ſignal was familiar, appeared
at the door. ALMORAN then commanded them to ſeize his brother, with
a countenance pale and livid, and a
voice

voice that was broken by rage. HA-
MET was ſtill unmoved; but ALMEI-
DA threw herſelf at the feet of ALMO-
RAN, and embracing his knees was about
to ſpeak, but he broke from her with
ſudden fury: ' If the world ſhould
' ſue,' ſaid he, ' I would ſpurn it off.
' There is no pang that cunning can
' invent, which he ſhall not ſuffer:
' and when death at length ſhall diſap-
' point my vengeance, his mangled
' limbs ſhall be caſt out unburied, to
' feed the beaſts of the deſert and the
' fowls of heaven.' During this menace, ALMEIDA ſunk down without
ſigns of life; and HAMET ſtruggling
in vain for liberty to raiſe her from the
ground, ſhe was carried off by ſome
women who were called to her aſ-
ſiſtance.

In

In this awful crifis, HAMET, who felt his own fortitude give way, looked up; and though he conceived no words, a prayer afcended from his heart to heaven, and was accepted by Him, to whom our thoughts are known while they are yet afar off. For HAMET, the fountain of ftrength was opened from above; his eye fparkled with confidence, and his breaft was dilated by hope. He commanded the guard that were leading him away to ftop, and they implicitly obeyed; he then ftretched out his hand towards ALMORAN, whofe fpirit was rebuked before him : ' Hear me,' faid he, ' thou tyrant! for it is thy genius that ' fpeaks by my voice. What has been ' the fruit of all thy guilt, but accu- ' mulated mifery ? What joy haft thou

' de-

' derived from undivided empire? what
' joy from the prohibition of my mar-
' riage with ALMEIDA? what good
' from that power, which some evil
' dæmon has added to thy own? what,
' at this moment, is thy portion, but
' rage and anguish, disappointment,
' and despair? Even I, whom thou
' seeft the captive of thy power, whom
' thou haft wronged of empire, and
' yet more of love; even I am happy,
' in comparison of thee. I know
' that my sufferings, however multi-
' plied, are short; for they shall end
' with life, and no life is long: then
' shall the everlasting ages commence;
' and through everlasting ages thy suf-
' ferings shall increase. The moment
' is now near, when thou shalt tread
' that line which alone is the path to
                              ' heaven,

' heaven, the narrow path that is
' ſtretched over the pit, which ſmokes
' for ever, and for ever! When thine
' aking eye ſhall look forward to the
' end that is far diſtant, and when be-
' hind thou ſhalt find no retreat ; when
' thy ſteps ſhall faulter, and thou ſhalt
' tremble at the depth beneath, which
' thought itſelf is not able to fathom ;
' then ſhall the angel of diſtribution
' lift his inexorable hand againſt thee :
' from the irremeable way ſhall thy
' feet be ſmitten ; thou ſhalt plunge in
' the burning flood ; and though thou
' ſhalt live for ever, thou ſhalt riſe no
' more.'

As the words of HAMET ſtruck AL-
MORAN with terror, and over-awed him
by an influence which he could not ſur-

mount ;

mount; HAMET was forced from his presence, before any other orders had been given about him, than were implied in the menace that was addressed to ALMEIDA: no violence, therefore, was yet offered him; but he was secured, till the king's pleasure should be known, in a dungeon not far from the palace, to which he was conducted by a subterraneous passage; and the door being closed upon him, he was left in silence, darkness, and solitude, such as may be imagined before the voice of the Almighty produced light and life.

When ALMORAN was sufficiently recollected to consider his situation, he despaired of prevailing upon ALMEIDA to gratify his wishes, till her attachment to HAMET was irreparably broken;

ken; and he, therefore, refolved to put him to death. With this view, he repeated the fignal, which convened the minifters of death to his prefence; but the found was loft in a peal of thunder that inftantly followed it, and the Genius, from whom he received the talifman, again ftood before him.

' ALMORAN,' faid the Genius, ' I
' am now compelled into thy prefence
' by the command of a fuperior power;
' whom, if I fhould dare to difobey,
' the energy of his will might drive me,
' in a moment, beyond the limits of
' nature and the reach of thought, to
' fpend eternity alone, without com-
' fort, and without hope.' ' And what,'
faid ALMORAN, ' is the will of this
' mighty and tremendous being?' ' His

' wiil,'

' will,' said the Genius, ' I will reveal
' to thee. Hitherto, thou haft been
' enabled to lift the rod of adverfity
' againft thy brother, by powers which
' nature has not entrufted to man: as
' thefe powers, and thefe only, have
' put him into thy hand, thou art for-
' bidden to lift it againft his life; if
' thou hadft prevailed againft him by
' thy own power, thy own power would
' not have been reftrained : to afflict
' him thou art ftill free; but thou art
' not permitted to deftroy. At the mo-
' ment, in which thou fhalt conceive
' a thought to cut him off by violence,
' the punifhment of thy difobedience
' fhall commence, and the pangs of
' death fhall be upon thee.' ' If then,'
said ALMORAN, ' this awful power
' is the friend of HAMET; what yet
' remains,

'. remains, in the ftores of thy wifdom,
' for me? 'Till he dies, I am at once
' precluded from peace, and fafety,
' and enjoyment.' ' Look up,' faid
the Genius, ' for the iron hand of de-
' fpair is not yet upon thee. Thou
' canft be happy, only by his death;
' and his life thou art forbidden to
' take away: yet mayft thou ftill arm
'.him againft himfelf; and if he dies by
' his own hand, thy wifhes will be full.'
' O name,' faid ALMORAN, ' but the
' means, and it fhall this moment be
' accomplifhed!' ' Select,' faid the Genius, ' fome friend—

At the name of friend, ALMORAN
ftarted and looked round in defpair.
He recollected the perfidy of Ofmyn;
and he fufpected that, from the fame

caufe,

caufe, all were perfidious: ' While ' HAMET has yet life,' faid he, ' I ' fear the face of man, as of a favage ' that is prowling for his prey.' ' Re- ' linquifh not yet thy hopes,' faid the Genius; ' for one, in whom thou wilt ' joyfully confide, may be found. Let ' him fecretly obtain admittance to ' HAMET, as if by ftealth; let him ' profefs an abhorrence of thy reign, ' and compaffion for his misfortunes; ' let him pretend that the rack is even ' now preparing for him; that death ' is inevitable, but that torment may ' be avoided: let him then give him ' a poignard, as the inftrument of de- ' liverance; and, perhaps, his own hand ' may ftrike the blow, that fhall give ' thee peace.' ' But who,' faid ALMO- RAN, ' fhall go upon this important ' errand?'

' errand?' ' Who,' replied the Genius,
' but thyfelf? Haft thou not the power
' to affume the form of whomfoever
' thou wouldft have fent?' ' I would
' have fent Ofmyn,' faid ALMORAN,
' but that I know him to be a traitor.'
' Let the form of Ofmyn then,' faid
the Genius, ' be thine. The fhadows
' of the evening have now ftretched
' themfelves upon the earth: com-
' mand Ofmyn to attend thee alone in
' the grove, where Solyman, thy fa-
' ther, was ufed to meditate by night;
' and when thy form fhall be impreffed
' upon him, I will there feal his eyes
' in fleep, till the charm fhall be
' broken; fo fhall no evil be at-
' tempted againft thee, and the trans-
' formation fhall be known only to
' thyfelf.'

ALMORAN,

ALMORAN, whofe breaft was again illuminated by hope, was about to exprefs his gratitude and joy; but the Genius fuddenly difappeared. He began, therefore, immediately to follow the inftructions that he had received: he commanded Ofmyn to attend him in the grove, and forbad every other to approach; by the power of the talifman he affumed his appearance, and faw him fink down in the fupernatural flumber before him: he then quitted the place, and prepared to vifit HAMET in the prifon.

C H A P.

CHAP. XVIII.

THE officer who commanded the guard that kept the gate of the prison, was Caled. He was now next in truft and power to Ofmyn: but as he had propofed a revolt to HAMET, in which Ofmyn had refufed to concur, he knew that his life was now in his power; he dreaded left, for fome flight offence, or in fome fit of caufelefs difpleafure, he fhould difclofe the fecret to ALMORAN, who would then certainly condemn him to death. To fecure this fatal fecret, and put an end to his inquietude, he refolved,

from

from the moment that ALMORAN was
eftablifhed upon the throne, to find
fome opportunity fecretly to deftroy
Ofmyn: in this refolution, he was confirmed by the enmity, which inferior
minds never fail to conceive againft
that merit, which they cannot but envy without fpirit to emulate, and by
which they feel themfelves difgraced
without an effort to acquire equal honour; it was confirmed alfo by the
hope which Caled had conceived, that,
upon the death of Ofmyn, he fhould
fucceed to his poft: his apprehenfions
likewife were increafed, by the gloom
which he remarked in the countenance
of Ofmyn; and which not knowing that
it arofe from fear, he imputed to jea-
loufy and malevolence.

When

When ALMORAN, who had now affumed the appearance of Ofmyn, had
paffed the fubterranean avenue to the
dungeon in which HAMET was confined,
he was met by Caled; of whom he demanded admittance to the prince, and
produced his own fignet, as a teftimony
that he came with the authority of
the king. As it was Caled's intereft to
fecure the favour of Ofmyn till an opportunity fhould offer to cut him off,
he received him with every poffible
mark of refpect and reverence; and
when he was gone into the dungeon,
he commanded a beverage to be prepared for him againft he fhould return,
in which fuch fpices were infufed, as
might expel the malignity which, in
that place, might be received with the
breath of life; and taking himfelf the

key

key of the prison, he waited at the
door.

. When ALMORAN entered the dungeon, with a lamp which he had received from Caled, he found HAMET
sitting upon the ground : his countenance was impressed with the characters of grief; but it retained no marks
either of anger or fear. When he
looked up, and saw the features of
Osmyn, he judged that the mutes were
behind him; and, therefore, rose up,
to prepare himself for death. ALMO-
RAN beheld his calmness and fortitude
with the involuntary praise of admiration; yet persisted in his purpose without remorse. ' I am come,' said he,
' by the command of ALMORAN, to ·
' denounce that fate, the bitterness of
which

' which I will enable thee to avoid.'
' And what is there,' faid HAMET,
' in my fortunes, that has prompted
' thee to the danger of this attempt ?'
' The utmoſt that I can give thee,'
faid ALMORAN, I can give thee with-
' out danger to myſelf: but though I
' have been placed, by the hand of for-
' tune, near the perſon of the tyrant,
' yet has my heart in ſecret been thy
' friend. If I am the meſſenger of
' evil, impute it to him only by whom
' it is deviſed. The rack is now pre-
' paring to receive thee; and every
' art of ingenious cruelty will be ex-
' hauſted to protract and to increaſe
' the agonies of death.' ' And what,'
faid HAMET, ' can thy friendſhip offer
' me?' ' I can offer thee,' faid ALMO-
RAN, ' that which will at once diſmiſs

thee

' thee to thofe regions, where the wick-
' ed ceafe from troubling, and the
' weary reft for ever.' He then produced the poignard from his bofom;
and prefenting it to HAMET, ' Take
' this,' faid he, ' and fleep in peace.'

HAMET, whofe heart was touched
with fudden joy at the fight of fo unexpected a remedy for every evil, did
not immediately reflect, that he was
not at liberty to apply it: he fnatched
it in a tranfport from the hand of AL-
MORAN, and expreffed his fenfe of the
obligation by clafping him in his arms,
and fhedding the tears of gratitude in
his breaft. ' Be quick,' faid ALMORAN:
' this moment I muft leave thee; and
' in the next, perhaps, the meffengers
' of deftruction may bind thee to the
' rack.'

‘ rack. ‘ I will be quick,’ said HA-
MET; ‘ and the figh that fhall laft
‘ linger upon my lips, fhall blefs thee.’
They then bid each other farewel:
ALMORAN retired from the dungeon,
and the door was again clofed upon
HAMET.

Caled, who waited at the door till
the fuppofed Ofmyn fhould return,
prefented him with the beverage which
he had prepared, of which he recounted
the virtues; and ALMORAN received it
with pleafure, and having eagerly drank
it off, returned to the palace. As
foon as he was alone, he refumed his
own figure, and fate, with a confident
and impatient expectation, that in a
fhort time a meffenger would be dif-
patched to acquaint him with the death
of

of Hamet. Hamet, in the mean time,
having grafped the dagger in his hand,
and raifed his arm for the blow, ' This,'
faid he, ' is my paffport to the realms
' of peace, the immediate and only
' object of my hope!' But at thefe
words, his mind inftantly took the
alarm: ' Let me reflect,' faid he, ' a
' moment: from what can I derive
' hope in death?—from that patient
' and perfevering virtue, and from that
' alone, by which we fulfill the tafk
' that is affigned us upon the earth.
' Is it not our duty, to fuffer, as well
' as to act? If my own hand configns
' me to the grave, what can it do but
' perpetuate that mifery, which, by
' difobedience, I would fhun? what
' can it do, but cut off my life and
' hope together?' With this reflec-

tion

tion he threw the dagger from him; and ftretching himfelf again upon the ground, refigned himfelf to the difpofal of the Father of man, moft Merciful and Almighty.

ALMORAN, who had now refolved to fend for the intelligence which he longed to hear, was difpatching a meffenger to the prifon, when he was told that Caled defired admittance to his prefence. At the name of Caled, he ftarted up in an extafy of joy; and not doubting but that HAMET was dead, he ordered him to be inftantly admitted. When he came in, ALMORAN made no enquiry about HAMET, becaufe he would not appear to expect the event, which yet he fuppofed he had brought about; he, therefore,

afked

afked him only upon what bufinefs he came. ' I come, my lord,' faid he, ' to ' apprize thee of the treachery of Of- ' myn.' ' I know,' faid ALMORAN, ' that Ofmyn is a traitor; but of ' what doft thou accufe him? ' As I ' was but now,' faid he, ' changing ' the guard which is fet upon HAMET, ' Ofmyn came up to the door of the ' prifon, and producing the royal fig- ' net demanded admittance. As the ' command which I received, when he ' was delivered to my cuftody, was ab- ' folute, that no foot fhould enter, I ' doubted whether the token had not ' been obtained, by fraud, for fome ' other purpofe; yet, as he required ad- ' mittance only, I complied: but that ' if any treachery had been contrived, ' I might deteft it; and that no arti-

' fice

' fice might be practifed to favour an
' efcape ; I waited myfelf at the door,
' and liftening to their difcourfe I over-
' heard the treafon that I fufpected.'
' What then,' faid ALMORAN, ' didft
' thou hear ?' A part of what was faid,'
replied Caled, ' efcaped me: but I
' heard Ofmyn, like a perfidious and
' prefumptuous flave, call ALMORAN
' a tyrant ; I heard him profefs an in-
' violable friendfhip for HAMET, and
' affure him of deliverance. What
' were the means, I know not ; but he
' talked of fpeed, and fuppofed that
' the effect was certain.'

ALMORAN, though he was ftill impatient to hear of HAMET ; and difcovered, that if he was dead, ,his death
was unknown to Caled ; was yet

not-

notwithftanding rejoiced at what he heard: and as he knew what Caled told him to be true, as the converfation he related had paffed between himfelf and HAMET, he exulted in the pleaf-ing confidence that he had yet a friend; the glooms of fufpicion, which had in-volved his mind, were diffipated, and his countenance brightened with com-placency and joy. He had delayed to put Ofmyn to death, only becaufe he could appoint no man to fucceed him, of whom his fears did not render him equally fufpicious: but having now found, in Caled, a friend, whofe fide-lity had been approved when there had been no intention to try it; and being impatient to reward his zeal, and to inveft his fidelity with that power, which would render his fervices moft important;

important; he took a ring from his own finger, and putting it upon that of Caled, ' Take this,' faid he, ' as ' a pledge, that to-morrow Ofmyn ' fhall lofe his head; and that, from ' this moment, thou art invefted with ' his power.'

Caled having, in the converfation between ALMORAN and HAMET, dif-cerned indubitable treachery, which he imputed to Ofmyn whofe appearance AL-MORAN had then affumed, eagerly feized the opportunity to deftroy him; he, therefore, not trufting to the event of his accufation, had mingled poifon in the bowl which he prefented to ALMO-RAN when he came out from HAMET: this, however, at firft he had refolved to conceal.

K 3

In

In confequence of his accufation, he fuppofed Ofmyn would be queftioned upon the rack; he fuppofed alfo, that the accufation, as it was true, would be confirmed by his confeffion; that whatever he fhould then fay to the prejudice of his accufer, would be difbelieved; and that when after a few hours the poifon fhould take effect, no inquifition would be made into the death of a criminal, whom the bowftring or the fcimitar would otherwife have been employed to deftroy. But he now hoped to derive new merit from an act of zeal, which ALMORAN had approved before it was known, by condemning his rival to die, whofe death he had already infured: ' May ' the wifhes of my lord,' faid he, ' be ' always anticipated; and may it be found,

' ‘ found, that whatever he ordains is
‘ already done: may he accept the zeal
‘ of his fervant, whom he has delight-
‘ ed to honour; for, before the light of
‘ the morning fhall return, the eyes of
‘ Ofmyn fhall clofe in everlafting
‘ darknefs.’

At thefe words, the countenance of
ALMORAN changed; his cheeks became pale, and his lips trembled:
‘ What then,’ faid he, ‘ haft thou
‘ done?’ Caled, who was terrified and
aftonifhed, threw himfelf upon the
ground, and was unable to reply. AL-
MORAN, who now, by the utmoft effort of his mind, reftrained his confufion and his fear, that he might learn
the truth from Caled without diffimulation or difguife, raifed him from the

K 4   ground

ground and repeated his enquiry. ' If
' I have erred,' said Caled, ' impute it
' not: when I had detected the trea-
' chery of Ofmyn, I was tranfported
' by my zeal for thee. For proof
' that he is guilty, I appeal now to
' himfelf; for he yet lives: but that
' he might not efcape the hand of
' juftice, I mingled, in the bowl I
' gave him, the drugs of death.'

At thefe words, ALMORAN, ftrik-
ing his hands together, looked upward in an agony of defpair and horror, and fell back upon a fofa that was
behind him. Caled, whofe aftonifhment was equal to his difappointment
and his fears, approached him with a
trembling though hafty pace; but as
he ftooped to fupport him, ALMO-

RAN

RAN fuddenly drew his dagger and ftabbed him to the heart; and repeated the blow with reproaches and execrations, till his ftrength failed him.

In this dreadful moment, the Genius once more appeared before him ; at the fight of whom he waved his hand, but was unable to fpeak. ' Nothing,' faid the Genius, ' that has happened to AL-
' MORAN, is hidden from me. Thy
' peace has been deftroyed alike by
' the defection of Ofmyn, and by the
' zeal of Caled : thy life may yet be
' preferved ; but it can be preferved
' only by a charm, which HAMET muft
' apply.' ALMORAN, who had raifed his eyes, and conceived fome languid hope, when he heard that he might yet
live ;

live; caft them again down in defpair,
when he heard that he could receive
life only from HAMET. ' From HA-
' MET,' faid he, ' I have already taken
' the power to fave me; I have, by
' thy counfel, given him the inftru-
' ment of death, which, by thy coun-
' fel alfo, I urged him to ufe : he re-
' ceived it with joy, and he is now
' doubtlefs numbered with the dead.'
' HAMET,' faid the Genius, ' is not
' dead; but from the fountain of vir-
' tue he drinks life and peace. If
' what I fhall propofe, he refufes to per-
' form, not all the powers of earth,
' and fea, and air, if they fhould com-
' bine, can give thee life : but if he
' complies, the death, that is now fuf-
' pended over thee, fhall fall upon his
' head; and thy life fhall be again de-
' livered

' livered to the hand of time.' ' Make
' hafte then,' faid ALMORAN, ' and
' I will here wait the event.' ' The
' event,' faid the Genius, ' is not dif-
' ftant; and it is the laft experiment
' which my power can make, either
' upon him or thee: when the ftar of
' the night, that is now near the ho-
' rizon, fhall fet, I will be with him.'

When ALMORAN was alone, he reflected, that every act of fupernatural
power which the Genius had enabled
him to perform, had brought upon him
fome new calamity, though it always
promifed him fome new advantage. As
he would not impute this difappointment to the purpofes for which he employed the power that he had received,
he indulged a fufpicion, that it proceeded

ceeded from the perfidy of the Being
by whom it was beſtowed ; in his mind,
therefore, he thus reaſoned with himſelf: ' The Genius, who has pretend-
' ed to be the friend of ALMORAN,
' has been ſecretly in confederacy with
' HAMET : why elſe do I yet ſigh in
' vain for ALMEIDA ? and why elſe did
' not HAMET periſh, when his life was
' in my power ? By his counſel, I per-
' ſuaded HAMET to deſtroy himſelf ;
' and, in the very act, I was betrayed
' to drink the potion, by which I ſhall
' be deſtroyed : I have been led on,
' from miſery to miſery, by ineffectual
' expedients, and fallacious hopes. In
' this criſis of my fate, I will not truſt,
' with implicit confidence, in another :
' I will be preſent at the interview of
' this powerful, but ſuſpected Being,
' with

' with HAMET; and who can tell, but
' that if I detect a fraud, I may be
' able to difappoint it: however pow-
' erful, he is not omnifcient; I may,
' therefore, be prefent, unknown and
' unfufpected even by him, in a form
' that I can chufe by a thought, to
' which he cannot be confcious.'

C H A P.

CHAP. XIX.

IN confequence of this refolution, ALMORAN, having commanded one of the foldiers of the guard that attended upon HAMET into an inner room of the palace, he ordered him to wait there till his return : then making faft the door, he affumed his figure, and went immediately to the dungeon ; where producing his fignet, he faid, he had received orders from the king to remain with the prifoner, till the watch expired.

As

As he entered without fpeaking, and without a light, HAMET continued ftretched upon the ground, with his face towards the earth; and ALMO-RAN, having filently retired to a remote corner of the place, waited for the appearance of the Genius.

The dawn of the morning now broke; and, in a few minutes, the prifon fhook, and the Genius appeared. He was vifible by a lambent light that played around him; and HAMET ftart-ing from the ground, turned to the vifion with reverence and wonder: but as the Omnipotent was ever prefent to his mind, to whom all beings in all worlds are obedient, and on whom alone he relied for protection, he was neither confufed nor afraid. 'HAMET,' faid

the

the Genius, ' the crisis of thy fate is
' near.' ' Who art thou,' said HAMET,
' and for what purpose art thou come?'
' I am,' replied the Genius, ' an inha-
' bitant of the world above thee; and
' to the will of thy brother, my pow-
' ers have been obedient : upon him
' they have not conferred happiness, but
' they have brought evil upon thee. It
' was my voice, that forbad thy mar-
' riage with ALMEIDA; and my voice,
' that decreed the throne to ALMO-
' RAN: I gave him the power to af-
' fume thy form; and, by me, the
' hand of oppreffion is now heavy upon
' thee. Yet I have not decreed, that
' he fhould be happy, nor that thou
' fhouldft be wretched : darkness as
' yet rests upon my purpose; but my
' heart in fecret is thy friend.' ' If
' thou

' thou art, indeed my friend,' faid
HAMET, ' deliver me from this prifon ;
' and preferve HAMET for ALMEIDA.'
' Thy deliverance,' faid the Genius,
' muft depend upon thyfelf. There
' is a charm, of which the power is
' great ; but it is by thy will only, that
' this power can be exerted.'

The Genius then held out towards
him a fcroll, on which the feal of fe-
ven powers was impreffed. ' Take,'
faid he, ' this fcroll, in which the myf-
' terious name of Orofmades is writ-
' ten. Invoke the fpirits, that refide
' weftward from the rifing of the fun ;
' and northward, in the regions of
' cold and darknefs : then ftretch out
' thy hand, and a lamp of fulphur, felf
' kindled, fhall burn before thee. In
' the fire of this lamp, confume that

‘ which I now give thee; and as the
‘ fmoke, into which it changes, fhall
‘ mix with the air, a mighty charm
‘ fhall be formed, which fhall defend
‘ thee from all mifchief : from that
‘ inftant, no poifon, however potent,
‘ can hurt thee; nor fhall any pri-
‘ fon confine : in one moment, thou
‘ fhalt be reftored to the throne, and to
‘ ALMEIDA ; and the Angel of death,
‘ fhall lay his hand upon thy brother; to
‘ whom, if I had confided this laft beft
‘ effort of my power, he would have fe-
‘ cured the good to himfelf, and have
‘ transferred the evil to thee.’

ALMORAN, who had liftened unfeen
to this addrefs of the Genius to HA-
MET, was now confirmed in his fufpicions, that evil had been ultimately intended againft him; and that he had
been

been entangled in the toils of perfidy, while he believed himſelf to be aſſiſted by the efforts of friendſhip: he was alſo convinced, that by the Genius he was not known to be preſent. HAMET, however, ſtood ſtill doubtful, and AL-MORAN was kept ſilent by his fears. ' Whoever thou art,' ſaid HAMET, ' the condition of the advantages which ' thou haſt offered me, is ſuch as it ' is not lawful to fulfill: theſe horrid ' rites, and this commerce with unholy ' powers, are prohibited to mortals in ' the Law of life.' ' See thou to that,' ſaid the Genius: ' Good and evil are ' before thee; that which I now offer ' thee, I will offer no more.'

HAMET, who had not fortitude to give up at once the poſſibility of ſe-

curing

curing the advantages that had been offered, and who was feduced by human
frailty to deliberate at leaft upon the
choice; ftretched out his hand, and re-
ceiving the fcroll, the Genius inftantly
difappeared. That which had been
propofed as a trial of his virtue, AL-
MORAN believed indeed to be an offer
of advantage; he had no hope, therefore, but that HAMET would refufe
the conditions, and that he fhould be
able to obtain the talifman, and fulfill
them himfelf: he judged that the mind
of HAMET was in fufpenfe, and was
doubtful to which fide it might finally
incline; he, therefore, inftantly affumed
the voice and the perfon of OMAR, that
by the influence of his council he
might be able to turn the fcale.

When

When the change was effected, he called HAMET by his name ; and HA-MET, who knew the voice, anfwered him in a tranfport of joy and wonder : ‘ My friend,’ faid he, ‘ my father ! ‘ in this dreary folitude, in this hour ‘ of trial, thou art welcome to my ‘ foul as liberty and life ! Guide me ‘ to thee by thy voice ; and tell me, ‘ while I hold thee to my bofom, how ‘ and wherefore thou art come ?’ ‘ Do ‘ not now afk me,’ faid ALMORAN : ‘ it is enough that I am here ; and ‘ that I am permitted to warn thee of ‘ the precipice, on which thou ftand- ‘ eft. It is enough, that concealed in ‘ this darknefs, I have overheard the ‘ fpecious guile, which fome evil de- ‘ mon has practifed upon thee.’ ‘ Is it ‘ then certain,’ faid HAMET, ‘ that

L 3 ‘ this

' this being is evil?' ' Is not that be-
' ing evil, faid ALMORAN,' ' who pro-
' pofes evil, as the condition of good?'
' Shall I then,' faid HAMET, ' renounce
' my liberty and life? The rack is now
' ready; and, perhaps, the next mo-
' ment, its tortures will be inevitable.'
' Let me afk thee then,' faid ALMO-
' RAN, ' to preferve thy life, wilt thou
' deftroy thy foul?' ' O! ftay,' faid
HAMET—' Let me not be tried too
' far! Let the ftrength of Him who is
' Almighty, be manifeft in my weak-
' nefs!' HAMET then paufed a few moments; but he was no longer in
doubt: and ALMORAN, who difbelieved and defpifed the arguments, by
which he intended to perfuade him to
renounce what, upon the fame condition, he was impatient to fecure for
himfelf,

himfelf, conceived hopes that he fhould
fucceed; and thofe hopes were inftantly
confirmed.' ' Take then,' faid HA-
MET, ' this unholy charm; and re-
' move it far from me, as the fands of
' Alai from the trees of Oman; left, in
' fome dreadful hour, my virtue may
' fail me, and thy counfel may be want-
' ing!' Give it me then,' faid ALMO-
RAN; and feeling for the hands of each
other, he fnatched it from him in an
extafy of joy, and inftantly refuming his
own voice and figure, he cried out,
' At length I have prevailed : and life
' and love, dominion and revenge, are
' now at once in my hand !'

HAMET heard and knew the voice
of his brother, with aftonifhment; but
it was too late to wifh that he had with-
held

held the charm, which his virtue would not permit him to ufe. ' Yet a few ' moments pafs,' faid ALMORAN, ' and ' thou art nothing.' HAMET, who doubted not of the power of the talifman, and knew that ALMORAN had no principles which would reftrain him from ufing it to his deftruction, refigned himfelf to death, with a facred joy that he had efcaped from guilt. ALMORAN then, with an elation of mind that fparkled in his eyes, and glowed upon his cheek, ftretched out his hand, in which he held the fcroll; and a lamp of burning fulphur was immediately fufpended in the air before him: he held the myfterious writing in the flame; and as it began to burn, the place fhook with reiterated thunder, of which every peal was more terrible and more loud.

loud. HAMET, wrapping his robe round him, cried out, ' In the Fountain of ' Life that flows for ever, let my life be ' mingled! Let me not be, as if I had ' never been; but ſtill conſcious of my ' being, let me ſtill glorify Him from ' whom it is derived, and be ſtill happy ' in his love!'

ALMORAN, who was abſorbed in the anticipation of his own felicity, heard the thunder without dread, as the proclamation of his triumph: ' Let ' thy hopes,' ſaid he, ' be thy por- ' tion; and the pleaſures that I have ' ſecured, ſhall be mine.' As he pronounced theſe words, he ſtarted as at a ſudden pang; his eyes became fixed, and his poſture immoveable; yet his ſenſes ſtill remained, and he perceived
the

the Genius once more to ftand before him. ' ALMORAN,' faid he, ' to the ' laft founds which thou fhalt hear, let ' thine ear be attentive! Of the fpirits ' that rejoice to fulfill the purpofe of ' the Almighty, I am one. To HA- ' MET, and to ALMORAN, I have been ' commiffioned from above : I have ' been appointed to perfect virtue, by ' adverfity ; and in the folly of her ' own projects, to entangle vice. The ' charm, which could be formed only ' by guilt, has power only to produce ' mifery: of every good, which thou, ' ALMORAN, wouldft have fecured by ' difobedience, the oppofite evil is thy ' portion ; and of every evil, which ' thou, HAMET, waft, by obedience, ' willing to incur, the oppofite good is ' beftowed upon thee. To thee, HA-

MET,

' MET, are now given the throne of
' thy father, and ALMEIDA. And thou,
' ALMORAN, who, while I fpeak, art
' incorporating with the earth, fhalt re-
' main, through all generations, a me-
' morial of the truths which thy life
' has taught !'

At the words of the Genius, the
earth trembled beneath, and above the
walls of the prifon difappeared : the figure of ALMORAN, which was har-
dened into ftone, expanded by degrees ;
and a rock, by which his form and at-
titude are ftill rudely expreffed, became
at once a monument of his punifhment
and his guilt.

Such are the events recorded by Ac-
MET, the defcendant of the Prophet,

and

and the preacher of righteoufnefs ! for, to ACMET, that which paffed in fecret was revealed by the Angel of inftruction, that the world might know, that, to the wicked, increafe of power is increafe of wretchednefs; and that thofe who condemn the folly of an attempt to defeat the purpofe of a Genius, might no longer hope to elude the appointment of the Moft High.

F I N I S.